Field Notes

A Life-Story

Sheila Clapkin

ISBN: 1-4196-7372-6

ISBN-13: 978-1419673726

**To my family ancient and present,
and to all my friends,
I am part of you.**

I enjoyed the process of writing this book as if it were a gala event, and each day, I felt as if I were dressed in the most beautiful jeweled evening gowns, even though actually on many occasions it was only pajamas and a robe. When I was a little girl, I told Uncle Irving Stone that I was also going to be a writer. He said, "Well then, stick the seat of your pants to the seat of a chair and write, write, write."

If you see any resemblance to anyone you know or think you know, in this story, you are mistaken. All characters are fictitious, but names can belong to anyone and life events sometimes can be so similar they appear to be just like yours.

A special thank you to Marge Stuart and Kathy Levin.

Field Notes

Moving

It had been foggy all summer in San Francisco, and on September 19, 1939; the sun broke through just as the sac of water burst from the body of my mother. Shortly thereafter, Sunshine Joy Epstein came into this world. How did the name Sunshine appear in the rather staid Epstein clan? My mother said she thought that having a child was like basking in joyous sunshine.

My mother had been very ill for fifteen years before she finally died. One day, early in her illness, my father called me in a panic to come quickly. I came to find my mother unconscious in a pool of blood. This episode was many years ago. An illness lasting over fifteen years assists you in building a certain amount of patience with the dying process. I thought that prolonged patience readies you for the end of the life of a loved one, but I found myself crying for my mother last night, so length of time and illness did not prepared me to lose my one and only mother. I tell you this because I want you to listen to me.

I called 911 and in the time it took for help to arrive, I had forgiven my mother all of the ills I thought she had done to me during our lives together, I also forgave all the hurts, psychological reverberations, her criticisms and all of the pain she had caused me by trying to have me be the best in the world. As forgiveness took over, I began to thank my mother for driving me across town on weekly visits to the orthodontist so that I can now openly smile at everyone. I thanked her for helping me get out of a relationship that was so wrong for me. I thanked her for reading her Emily Post out loud and teaching me to look like a queen at the dinner table. I thanked her for helping me with a very arduous report on Israel full of pictures and statements of knowledge that produced an A+. I want you to understand that in forgiving my mother, in those few seconds surrounded by vomit and blood, any pain she may have caused me lifted, my scars smoothed out, and my cuts and abrasions ceased to exist. I was free to be my own invention. So, if you understand that you can live again whole in a new way by forgiveness, I want you to do it. I want you to be free of some of the shackles you have allowed others to put on you and of the ones you have inadvertently put there yourself.

When we moved to the San Fernando Valley in 1969, I felt it was my duty to our children to sign up for a temple and become immersed in Jewish life. I was politely told that I would have to be put on a waiting list. I was stunned into writing my first letter to God. I said, "God, this is news to me that I would have to be on a waiting list to be Jewish. Please, get me a deal."

I am ashamed of something I did. I lit candles in churches during my travels and said prayers for many things and many people I knew. Please forgive me, but I just found out I am supposed to pay for those candles, each and every one of them. I don't know how to make it up to so many different places in so many different corners of the earth. It was time to write my second letter to God.

I am Sunshine Epstein and I want to tell you something. Sunshine is my real name, but I had many other names attached to me. I wanted to be a writer, but worried that I might offend someone. I assumed names like Orchid Abowitz, Honey Riverton, Sonia Velasquez, Astral, Rose, David and others so if I said something that offended you, I wouldn't have to take responsibility for it because after all, it was one of my alter egos that said it, not me.

Last week I picked up my six-year-old grandson from school for one of our adventures. We talked about getting him a secret box with a combination lock on it. We went to Franklins Hardware store, we went to Rudy's Ace Hardware store, we went to Target and we could not find a box with a built in combination lock. He said to me, "Well, grandma, are you going to give up?"

"No, I am not. I never give up." I want you to know that I am a grandmother, but I wasn't always a grandmother and had a long time to live and wait to be one. I used my time waiting without the benefit of lessons in patience.

I wanted to be a grandmother before my children were even grown. I think it is because I wanted more children and my children held the tickets. Being given the exalted position of grandmother brings me to the belief that God has forgiven me for being perpetually on a waiting list, never joining a temple, for stealing candles to pray, lying to the principal about peeing in the school auditorium, and lifting that orange and white ice cream bar from the State Street Market.

My grandson and I bought three combination locks in different sizes and shapes with different numbers. We did not give up but decided to look for the lock box another day. We worked for hours on learning the right, left, right sequences and attaching the right numbers in the right spots. He was determined to learn the process. He finally got one lock open and said, "See, I didn't give up."

Have you given up? Don't. There is so much more that you do not know, that I do not know, that you want to know, and I want to know. I want you to know more about how it happened for me and remember, "Timing has a lot to do with the outcome of a the rain dance."

It was late in the summer of 1962 and I was moving. My pain was too great to stay here any longer. Fields' sister, Eugenia, was talking to me in hollow tones I could not decipher; I heard a buzzing in my ears, and my head felt like it was filled with foggy webs. I wanted to be alone but didn't want to hurry my lost friend's sister.

I pulled clothes out of drawers, rolling them in balls, and stuffing them into two shiny new suitcases. I fumbled among my clothing, discarding things I knew I was never going to see again. I scowled at the task, emptying the remaining drawers, attacking the closet floor with resolve. I decided to leave bits and pieces of myself here in my parents' home in hopes that my essence would not be gone forever.

I pulled myself into the moment. Fields was dead, gone from us.

Eugenia said, "Fields died instantly from a blow to the head."

"How do you know?"

"Investigators came to the house."

"Did they question you?"

"They questioned all of us."

"What did they want to know?"

"They wanted to know a little more about Fields. They actually think he was caught up in unsavory things. That's what they said, unsavory."

"What did they mean, unsavory?" I asked.

"Criminal activities, that's unsavory, right?"

"Did they say what kind?"

"No, but some guys he knew are doing bad things."

"Bad thing--what does that mean?"

"I don't know," Eugenia replied, "but they wanted to know if he had large amounts of cash with him, and I said I didn't know. They named some guys I didn't know."

"Did they ever come back and let you know what they found out?"

"They came to tell Mom that Fields died from a blow to the left side of his head, but they never came back after that."

What Eugenia did not know, I knew. Fields was in some kind of a quarrel with Tooty, but I thought it was kid stuff, like it used to be when he and some of his buddies would get into spats. He did carry lots of cash in the months before he was killed, but that was because his job in Seattle was a good one.

Fields wrote to me on many occasions about his job in Seattle and all that he was learning. He said that through his observations, he could be sure nothing was ever created, designed, and completed in a committee. He noticed that in a committee, while all looked quite collegial, one person took hold of the reigns and did the job, made the report, and disseminated the information to the rest of the firm. So his big claim to fame, according to him, was, "No great thing was ever done in a committee."

He asked me to find out if any other great human being had said this before him, and, if not, would I add the quotation marks and his name. After searching many spaces and places, I found only Fields has said this, so: "No great thing was ever done in a committee."–Fields.

Fields began his career at a top firm in the United States at that time, or so it seemed to me. He signed on with a very prestigious architectural firm based out of Seattle. His jobs were mainly to be situated in Seattle, but the company was planning to go global. Fields had always been a forward thinker and collected postcards of the most modern, futuristic buildings around the world.

His collection included late 19ᵗʰ Century and 20ᵗʰ Century postcards as well, but his favorites were those showing modern use of glass, steel, and grids that used the natural light as a base of form.

His firm had fingers stretching to major downtown areas, department stores, art galleries, dress shops, and renovations of some famous streets. Fields himself headed a department called Prefab Architecture. It was new, and he was working on how to add his love of modern high-tech designs into prefab opportunities. He always wondered how he became assigned to this department when none of his applications and none of the interview questions mentioned prefabricated architecture. It was new on the horizon, so no one thought to mention it.

Fields was responsible for the first design of a prefab garden shed. He took into consideration that most garden sheds have very low rooflines, and in his designs he expanded the roof to allow for much more storage as well as headroom. He figured that the people installing this shed would be placing a small architectural structure where it could be viewed from the main house. He designed all angles to possess a secret beauty, accessed by the viewer at whatever angle it was placed. He built in a peg-board on one of the walls, making it easier to store garden tools. He planned for a grid-patterned door to be included, as well as a window and an optional window box for seasonal flowers. It has been years since Fields died, but his prefab garden shed design is still being used with added variations. Just before he died, Fields had been working on a steel prefab garage, and he left the plans, nearly completed, neatly on the left side of his desk. They were found there after he passed and were completed by another young architect and submitted for approval that next week.

I mention that the documents were placed on the left side of his desk because I want you to know that Fields was left-handed. I want you to picture us together and how we were when we would lie down next to each other. I want you to know how our energy flowed into each other. Facing out, Fields was always on the right side and I on the left. His left hand would be into me and my right hand would be into him. Our energy flowed best that way, his left into my right, and my right into his left.

Somehow, in the hour before he was killed, I knew

Fields was coming to see me. I knew he wanted me to help him. If only things could have been different, if I could have been somewhere else, stayed home somehow; then he would not have been on that street, murdered. I was left with the only thing I know how to do. I will keep Fields inside the fabric of my life and keep the best of him alive.

The work that I did in the Upper Haight area has remained a well-guarded secret. I didn't talk about it much because I thought if no one knew about it, they wouldn't expect my success and would not know about any failures. Remember, I even used pen names to write so I wouldn't have to take responsibility for anything I wrote. I do not feel that way now, but then was a different time. No one really asked questions; they just accepted that I did some writing. Why did I stay even after I received my teaching credential? I stayed because I loved the writing and the challenge of each new project.

What happens in a life that makes it worth writing about? When I think of my friend Fields' life, I think of past remembrances that sway and buckle like a weeping wind. They puff and bluster hardily, swooping up bits of debris as they go. They land somewhere, but I can't find them. If I found them, would I be able to put Fields back together again? He was gone, my salvation, my anchor, my treasured love. I worried that I might never, ever again find the happiness and the easy relationship I had with Fields.

House On Downey Street

"LIFE IS SIMPLER WHEN YOU PLOW AROUND THE STUMP."

I sat fully dressed in my studio on Downey Street in one of the oldest houses in the city. The stairs leading up to the doors were crumbling, I had puttied and painted them over, but the telltale signs of a hundred years of wear and tear were still there. The large inserted piece of stained glass above the door had tiny cracks in the corners, but it was still as beautiful as the first day the old house was inhabited. In fact, the glass was ordered and designed by my great-great grandparents.

Entering the Downey Street house, your eyes first

noticed the oversized living room and the dining room on the downstairs floor. You could see through the entryway and into the cheerfully painted kitchen. The yellow and white embroidered curtains would blow lightly in the wind, starched and ironed so expertly that they showed no age at all. In reality, you could say they were as old as the house; they were here when Isaac and Rachel raised their family, they were here when Max and Ida raised theirs, they were here when Dora and Joe raised theirs, when Stanley and Ruth raised theirs, and Marty and Rose raised theirs. They were still there when I left to make my rounds in the neighborhood, which always gave me a sense of other lives and a surrounding of good will.

Every weekday morning, I walked to Frederick Street, veered right, and headed one block over to Ashbury, then made a left to reach Haight. Upper Haight was where I was headed. My neighborhood was the corner of Haight and Ashbury, now the most famous intersection in the world. My family lived on Downey Street for generations, and back in the 60s the adjoining neighborhoods had become the birthplace of the hippie counterculture whose actions and ideals inspired and continue to inspire generations of freethinkers. Today you can still see tourists who come to view it and are pleased not only by the beautiful Victorian homes that surround the area, but also by the many unusual shops and colorful characters living in the district as well as on the street. But now, there are two very different areas of the district--Upper Haight, a moneyed shopping area stretching to Golden Gate Park, and Lower Haight, a more diverse neighborhood containing a nightlife zone.

I was headed for Upper Haight. The tickets for that evening's flight to Los Angeles had been a long time in coming. I always knew I would have to go, but not when. Time on my old life had run out and I was ready. The only person who could have gone with me was Fields, and he was already gone.

Fields and I had grown up together in homes whose sides matched; our bedroom windows, exactly--same height and width, were placed precisely opposite each other. I think back to the times when I would look for him in the window, and he was usually there. Never again would I find the perfect window partner. Sunshine and Fields, Fields and Sunshine a twosome when twosomes were reserved for older couples. We shared most moments of our early childhood and had endless days together. We had pure, unconditional love for each other.

A heartrending tragedy struck our companionship when Fields' parents decided to move uptown and thus separated the perfect pair. The days leading up to the move were intense, and the day of the move and the empty window nearly unbearable. I think that episode was responsible for all of my emotional upheavals from that time on. I sat for hours and days watching the empty window. Rarely if ever did I even see a shadow cross its frame. I was lonely and learned forever about love lost and loneliness. I just didn't know how to ease the pain. As the months passed, we found ways to spend time together. We found a way to meet halfway between our homes and still enjoy a deep camaraderie and love.

Fields loved the things that made me happy. Together we loved to walk with the sun on our backs, hiking long hours in the country, coming back to our city streets renewed and full of each other. We talked about limitless possibilities and realized that there are some limitations, astral, human, natural and societal. We read poems to each other, sampling words from Edgar Allan Poe,

James Joyce, and Robert Frost.

Fields captured my imagination by outlining the incredibly long journey to Nirvana and the fact that one must live endless circles of lifetimes; thus, we discussed and re-discussed reincarnation. Fields felt that this path and its stages would confuse the devil and do right by him. We spent the next fifteen years traveling to and from each other, in and out of each other's heads, joining bodies, touching spirits, kindling and dousing flames, conceptualizing, analyzing, evaluating and synthesizing truths, tales, wishes, dreams and other things.

For The Love Of Fields

■■■ ■■

*"WHEN YOU'RE THROWING YOUR NAME AROUND, BE READY
TO HAVE IT THROWN AROUND BY SOMEBODY ELSE."*

During my walk on Fredrick Street that particular day, the wind blew so hard across the Bay that my hair whipped forward, preceding me. I always had a hair fetish. I always put off getting haircuts because of the terrible trauma for months preceding the cut. Once I saw Jean Simmons in a movie and her hair was short with little spikes in front. I had my hair cut exactly the same as hers only it didn't quite look as good on me as it did on her. They boys in school put their hands in their shirts and called me "Little Napoleon". I never quite got over that and am still fighting the hair fetish. Either it is too long or too short. Lots of friends and relatives have always had something to say about the way I should or shouldn't wear my hair. Now I don't care.

I hesitated before entering the poorly lit storefront, my feet scraping the pavement and spreading accumulated leaves, papers and bits of the days and nights that came and went before I stood here. I hung my coat on the rack and smiled hello to everyone, knowing this was not a regular day.

Beyond those doors lay a large cave-like room with a damp, musty smell. To me it always seemed like a breath of fresh air, but in reality it bordered on being a stench. Work was being done there, the kind of work that emanated from your soul, deeply engrained with heart, lung and brain tissue. My ears filled with the clicking, buzzing, whirring sounds as I took my place. My machine was my private domain; my cubical was my space, my ideas stemmed from observations from my lifetime of living.

I wrote articles for *Ace Vintage*, a magazine dedicated to all that happened from the early 1900's to present time. That week I was assigned a piece on The Art Deco Era and how it continued to affect our culture in the 20th Century. "Art Deco was and still is an elegant style of decorative art, design and architecture," I began, and then got distracted by the realization that Art Deco replaced the style of Art Nouveau, which is also quite elegant and decorative. "Art Nouveau was popular until around the time of World War I and was then replaced by Art Deco," I continued. The article stopped there.

I left it, my last article for *Ace Vintage,* in the middle of the desk, knowing I would not be back. I understood that leaving San Francisco, my family remnants, my work on the magazine and all the San Francisco memories, and the familiar sights that reminded me of Fields, would be a challenge. Los Angeles had its similarities, but mostly it would be different. Marilynn was there. Marilynn would help. When you have a sister, you have a tremendous treasure or a barely bearable burden; to me there was little in between. Marilynn was my sister.

My love for Fields came so easily; it came on wisps of air, like a gift from the sea, like an enormous ice cream cone that you lick and lick until it is gone. Fields was gone, like the ice cream and the cone; the memory of it was so good, but eaten and now gone.

Love has always held pain for me; a memory reminds me of how I made a decision about love. We were in a carpool, three girls, mother and I. One of the girls was lamenting how it hurts to lose a boyfriend. She had been dating the football star of a neighboring high school and when she went to his game, he told her to wait for him in front of the school after the game. Darkness descended and she was frightened, so she called her uncle to come and get her. From her uncle's car as they were driving away, she spotted her boyfriend looking for her. That evening he called and said he could not trust someone who would not wait for him, even in the dark. Her new love was not a love anymore.

"I know how you feel." said my mother

"You do?"

"I do, I have lost loves."

My ears perked in their direction, anxious to know a secret my mother might reveal.

My mother was quiet for a moment, then almost inaudibly she said, "When I was in the sixth grade, the teacher quoted from Samuel Butler, "It is better to have loved and lost then to never have loved at all."

It was quiet for the rest of our ride because we were all pondering this singular quotation, one with tentacles and side roads, and it made me realize there was no price I wasn't willing to pay for love.

Dear Fields, goodbye, but only until I think clearly again.

Seeded

"LIFE'S THE ONLY EXPERIMENT THAT CANNOT FAIL."

Here I was, seeded and born in San Francisco, now heading for Los Angeles. I felt like I was kicked out of town, but in reality I kicked myself out. I left the old place on Downey Street, Dad and Mom, the old neighborhood and all that I had known. I asked Eugenia to watch after Mom and Dad for me. Mom's illness was hard for dad and he said he had faced it for so long that he knew what to do. I made certain that they had help in their home and increased the help, as it was needed.

Fields always said that I would make it anywhere because I have the gift. What gift? I struggled to know what he knew. Now that I had formulated the questions, he was not there to answer them. One time he told me that I am talented and I should share my talents with the world. Another thing I remember him telling me was that he was sure we would both become famous, but that we would have to wait until we were dead. The first one of us was dead, so did that make us half famous?

It was good to be leaving the grounds of past prejudice. My parents thought I should go to Brockley School, which eventually turned into a college preparatory school. It was the sophisticated school uptown. Did my parents know that I would be the only Jewish girl anyone had ever seen? Did they know that I would be target practice for future anti-semites? They had many clubs in that preparatory school: band, orchestra leadership, the chess club, the radio club, varsity baseball, varsity swimming, gymnastics, tennis, cross country, varsity football, the letterman, future engineers of America, future teachers of America, future medics, future hostesses of America, but the club with the most members was the future anti-semites of America. No one from this club had their pictures taken for preservation in the annual book of memories and no one from this club even knew they were members. Did I have good times growing up Jewish? Oh yes, but I strongly remember the ones that hurt. I always wondered about my name, Sunshine Epstein. As I see it now, it was a dead give away as to the origins of the person carrying this name.

My time of reverie came to an end as the plane landed and taxied to a stop. The walk from the plane to the arrival area had my heart in an uproar because Marilynn was never on time. Surprise! Marilynn was there to pick me up to begin my life in Los Angeles; she was on time. My luggage fit perfectly into the back seat of her little red car and we headed for her apartment.

It did not take me long to understood the living arrangements Marilynn had figured out for us. I learned all I needed to know on the ride from the airport to the apartment. I was to share all of the expenses with her until I got on my feet. Marilynn and I were not in the same age grouping, so she had completely different friends when we were younger. Four years makes a huge difference in the growing-up stages. Also, even though our biological beginnings happened from the same genetic structures, we were not the same in any other respects.

Being with Marilynn reminded me that my friends' mothers would not let their little angels play with me, probably because of the boys in our house. Maybe Marilynn's friends were more careful about the stories they went home with; they chose our house to visit and to enjoy. I think they rather liked the parade of young men in our home. They were the right age for boy interests. My mother used to take in boys from the city's home for boys. Maybe she had some altruistic motives, but I thought of it as a cheap means of securing all kinds of services, like babysitting. Marilynn, her girlfriends and I had our eyes and ears filled with the ways of boys through the presence of those lads from the home. I developed young and had a chest full of swollen mammary glands by the time I was eleven.

I remember one particular boy I called Snot Nose because he always had a snotty nose; looking back, I wish I could have slipped him some antibiotics. He would have been cured of his snotty nose, but not of his boob fetish. I am confident that he carries that fetish with him today if he hasn't croaked. He used to eye me up and down and finally settle on my bosom. Every time he would go by me, he would either pinch, poke, pop, pat, bump, rub, graze, bite, pick, pluck, swipe at or nudge my breasts.

"Hey, Marilynn, do you remember Snot Nose?"

"Sure I do. God, what is making you think of him now?"

"Just was. Did he ever poke at your boobs?"

"No, honey, he never did; none of those boys even looked at me. Do you remember Sophie? She used to drool over them, but I didn't like any of them. Hey, I hope you don't mind cramped quarters. It won't be so bad because I am usually out. I don't even come home to sleep every night."

"You don't"

"Well, little Sunshine, if you are lucky, you won't be coming home every night either."

The apartment was brightly lit as you entered the living room, but the further back you went, the smaller, darker and more airless the rooms became. I was struck by the smallness of the room we both would share. It had no significance when she first said it, but I became very glad that Marilynn wasn't planning on being home very many nights.

I put my things in a corner of the room, and began taking clothes out of the suitcase; but realizing that
Marilynn was standing there watching me and smiling, I
put them back again. "You know you can do that any-
time–lets talk," she said. She was right; I could arrange my
things when she wouldn't be there.

Marilynn prepared tea, and we began to share memories of our childhood.

"Remember, Sunshine, when they wouldn't let you
join the Rainbow Girls because they said you were the
wrong race?"

"Those shits–they couldn't get away with that these
days," I said.

"They can and they do."

Marilynn continued. "Listen, when Grandma died,
I got her Eastern Star ring. I thought this was the greatest
gift and immediately applied to join. Three ladies came to
the house on Downey Street. We sat and talked over apple
pie and ice cream. It was about the most all-American
thing I could think of at the time. I told them I wanted to
join their organization and serve as Grandma had done."

"You never told me."

"I know, because I felt ashamed and angry. They didn't call back, so I called them. The lovely, but high-pitched voice on the other end said, 'Well, dear, we think you are just fantastic with all of the things you are doing, but we think you should join the bethel of your kind in the downtown area. You know, I hung up the receiver, but not before I disgraced our so-called race. I gave her a string of cuss words uttered, until then, only by drunken sailors. The next day I went to the bridge and threw the ring into the ocean's depths. Sometimes I think of that ring, and all of its significance, at the bottom of the sea."

Marilynn seemed exasperated and lost in a spatial kind of stare. Finally, she sighed with seeming relief and said, "Your turn for the next story."

I searched back into my memory and a flash of myself sitting in that sun soaked room lit up my senses. "I remember when I was in the fourth grade," I said. "I was called to the principal's office and was told that I would be moving to another class. He said he was moving me to this new class because I would fit in better. He said that I had called one of the boys in my present class a son of a gun. I told him that I didn't know guns had sons.

His eyes widened, the veins in his neck popped out and then his eyes became steely. He said, "Don't act like a smart aleck with me, young lady. Buckle up your mouth." He stood up and removed his belt in a swashbuckling movement that scared me more than I realized. He swung his belt around and around, and then he said, "If I hear anymore trouble about you, I'm going to use this thing.

He swung and snapped that belt until everything went black. All I remember is that I was told I had fainted. For years and years I had nightmares about belt swinging, dreadful guys with veins popping out on their necks and steely eyes staring at me.

When I actually walked into that new class I knew immediately I was in the wrong place. Characters like Jester Sharkey, Gary Olsen, and Mike Holms stared me down. Joyce Adler, Darla Benton, Joan Anderson and Gail Binge, looked at me with apprehension in their eyes. What could they do? What could I do? This was the troubled class, and now I was one of them. I missed my best friend Rosanne. She was so kind and loved me as much as I loved her. When we had lined up for class, she used to be there at recess time we used to sit together, and at lunchtime we used to share our treats. We talked effortlessly with each other, talk that was full of honesty and trust.

My old class with Rosanne in it lined up in a different place and played in different areas of the playground. My new class played at the opposite end of the yard. A number of times Roseanne and I were benched because we were in each other's play areas. I missed Rosanne. I still do. I miss the openness and the unconditional friendship that you can spend a lifetime looking for and never achieve." I told Marilynn that Roseanne later had a child and died of a brain tumor. We met for dinner after we had both been married about ten years. We enjoyed our conversation and promised to meet again.

"Years and years later, after we had gone on to another school, Mama had luncheon with one of the teachers, Mrs. Jones. She remained friendly with her until she died. Mrs. Jones asked Mama how I was doing and said she felt sorry about what happened to me. Mama asked, 'What happened to her?' I never told mama about the trouble and the class change because I thought she would stop loving me, stop because I had been singled out as trouble.

Mrs. Jones explained that Dr. and Mrs. Russell did not like the friendship I had with their daughter Roseanne. They wanted me removed to another class so that we would be separated, hoping this would help to disengage us from our attachment. They donated a film projector, a pull-down screen, and the deed was done. They absolutely did not want their precious daughter, light of their lives, to associate with the filth of my kind. So in retrospection, it wasn't that I called anyone a son of a gun, but in fact what I represented.

Marilyn, you know this left its mark on me physically and mentally, but it was fodder for a composition I wrote in my senior year. I won a prize for that one. I remember today what I wrote about then. I retold the story about the principal's office and recounted the origins of the phrase, son of a gun. I wrote that after sailors had crossed the Atlantic and they made it to the West Indies, they would be anxious for female companionship. Then, they would take the native women on the ship and have their way with them in between the cannons. Some of the women the sailors left behind would have boys, who were called sons between the guns. I did not mention the prejudice or the bigotry of Dr. and Mrs. Russell. I have the winning certificate for this essay on top of an even more faded one that says, Best One-Piece Bathing Suit. Those are my best shots, Marilynn."

"Oh, Sunshine, we have both had such vexations over this kind of thing. I really didn't realize it then, but I see it clearly now. It hurt back then, not so much now that I understand it. You had it worse than I did because you wanted so much more of people."

"Marilynn, I had it worse because I was the only Jewish person many of these people ever had contact with and they had been told by their mamas and their papas to check my forehead for horns and to see if my teeth were really green. Remember?

In Those Days

■■■ ■■

"DON'T SQUAT WITH YOUR SPURS ON."

Marilynn and I could talk all night long when we got the chance, just remembering things as we knew them or, so it turned out, how we thought we remembered them. Isn't it funny how we remember things that kept us in the spotlight or kept us looking innocent of the little crimes we all felt guilty remembering? I decided if Marilynn was willing and had the time, I would pour my memories out for her and relish her attention to them.

Lost in the moment, the quietness slipped both Marilynn and me into our own daydreams. I lapsed into a time when Fields and I talked about being different in the outside world, but being whole together. I remember him telling me of some obstacles he had to climb, but not in absolute detail. He had trouble with girls liking him as much as they liked his older brother and older cousins. He began his life shorter than most boys, and that aspect was the wedge separating him, life, and early acceptance.

Marilynn pierced my daydream with a question.

"Sunshine, do you remember the time you asked Guy Hendrickson to a dance? He said he really liked you and you were his dream girl come true, but he would be on everyone's hit list if he showed up with your kind. Remember, he wrote you such adoring notes and you were on top of the clouds. You didn't go to the dance, but spent the evening with the girls having dinner and talking."

I added that I still have his notes to me somewhere in my old white and gold jewelry box. Guy was another one who died young. He died in a plane crash on his way to join his football team in a play-off game. He stayed home to help his grandmother and told the team that he would take a later flight. His plane went down on the San Luis Obispo county line.

"Is it just coincidental that they are dead now--our silent accusers become our fearful, anxious companions hereafter? Is religion a race? Were these people from the hills? Did they really think I was dirty, had horns and green teeth? How could they think that I didn't take baths and was dirty? They were so harsh and accusatory. They wouldn't let me join them in the Jobs Daughters, the Rainbow Girls or the Brownies because they hated my kind. What kind am I? Did they really think I had any part whatsoever in nailing Jesus to that cross? Who are these people who nailed me to the cross of expulsion, exclusion, removal and ejection from the society around me? Are you still listening, Marilynn?"

"Yes, sure, go on. I kind of think you're on a roll that has been stuck for a long time. Really, go on."

I lapsed into silence but memories continued tumbling through my head. I clearly remember about three or four years after graduation, I was actually invited to a wedding of one of the girls from my hometown. By then I was away at the university. I was a nervous wreck, tense and uneasy, as all of us are when we have to face a reunion. I didn't know whether I would rather be hit by a

Mack truck or go to the wedding.

I had learned the art of makeup and hair design at the university, so I felt confident that I would look okay. I had the shock of my lifetime as I entered the reception hall where the wedding was being held. Everyone who I thought in those growing-up years was strikingly beautiful was not. Actually, they looked washed out and tired. They looked as if they had worked hard and spent all their time being angry for a lifetime. This was the group of girls, now women, who were in the class, the good class that I had been removed from in elementary school.

They still barricaded me from the group, but since my eyes had cleared, I saw the barricade not only as an emotional one but a physical one as well. They were all sitting in a horseshoe. I waved and motioned that I was coming over. These appallingly anti-semitic women had pulled empty chairs in a line across the open end of their self-imposed horseshoe with the backsides facing out, daring me not to sit down. They glared and shielded themselves as if I were carrying the pandemic of the century.

The men on the other hand looked their approval and had the wherewithal to approach and flirt. Bless them, for they do not know what they do–and did for me.

Darla, a sweet friend from the new class, the trouble class, came over to me and said, "I'm sure glad to see you have grown up, Sunshine. I'm shocked to see that they still act like that."

"Thank you Darla, I must have forgotten those years."

"No one forgets those years, but now you can recognize them for who they are. You are way ahead of them."

"I used to want to be them, like them, be liked by them."

"They aren't your friends, they never were, can't be. That much you should remember."

"Thanks Darla. I needed you to tell me that."

"I need to tell you to forget them, but remember them, too. Know what I mean?"

"I know, right."

That wedding day was a great day for me and the first day of my growth and development as the unadulterated, uncontaminated, unpolluted, untainted, wholesome woman I was then and more of what I was to become. Bless the invitation to the wedding for its salvation of my mind, my body and my soul.

I didn't tell Marilynn about my reoccurring moments with Fields. I will call them strange experiences. Fields would come back to be with me during quiet times. He came to me in rolling balls of air, as a misty moment, hair blowing or a hand on my back. It never scared me once I realized it was Fields. It sometimes came as a firm pressure of a hand on my back, a hello and a good bye. One time he contacted me as I was walking in and around Marilynn's apartment. I could actually see him, feel his arm up against my shoulder and the warmth was startling. I began answering questions that were not asked as if I knew what he would want to know. "Yes, I am fine, but I miss you. I remember the time we danced in the park. Yes, I would like that. Yes, I can call your sister Eugenia. Your mom is fine. My mom is the same. Tooty? Tooty is fine. I know you know about the celebrations. They are for you."

Around Marilynn's Apartment

■ ■ ■ ■ ■

*"GENERALLY YOU AREN'T LEARNING ANYTHING WHEN
YOUR MOUTH'S MOVING."*

After several days of familiarizing myself by walking the immediate environment and then venturing out to ride the public transports, I learned many new neighborhoods in and around Marilynn's apartment. I used public transit to apply at several employment agencies while waiting for my papers and credentials to clear the educational system. I needed a temporary job to tide me over while awaiting my appointment to a teaching position.

Within an hour of returning to the apartment, I received a call from one of the agencies to immediately go to Signal's Cigar Factory because they were looking for someone to fill a part-time position. I arrived promptly and Phil, who seemed to be in charge, ushered me into the establishment. Close your eyes and picture this--wood floors, wood panels, wooden desks, wooden filing cabinets, and wooden chairs, plus wooden stairways leading to an enormous upstairs factory. Was Phil smoking a cigar? Oh yes. You would think that surrounded by all that wood, smoking would be forbidden.

He showed me to a desk; wooden of course, which was located next to twenty or more filing cabinets. He explained, all the while blowing little puffs from his cigar right at me, that he needed to change his filing system. It was hard to duck the smoke puffs for fear he would think I was spastic. He continued to explain that the files were out of date and needed to be updated, plus he wanted new crispy looking file covers so that when he opened them, they looked important.

"Now, little lady, is there anything more you think you need to know before you get to work?"

"No, Phil, thank you."

"Lunch is at noon, breaks are 10:00 and 2:30.

Sound fair?"

"Very good, Phil."

I barreled through the first cabinet. I looked through the others. I had a great idea of filing and cross-filing, but every time I tried to tell Phil my plan, he was busy. I just went ahead and did what I thought would be great. Break time came, lunchtime came, another break came, and I didn't look up from my work for even one minute. A sweat rose and dried on the skin of my arms and belly several times during the day, but I was steadfast. At quitting time, I had arranged and rearranged that filing system, and when Phil came to check my progress, the files sparkled and twinkled as he opened each of the 80 drawers. I explained the cross-filing system I had installed for him, and he smiled.

"My, my, little lady, you have done a fine job. You can pick up your check for the day from Mrs. Lodden in the office before you leave. Let me just tell you something, Miss Sunshine. This job was for the week. You could have stretched it out all week and received a week's pay for the same work. No one expected anyone could get the job done in one day. Let me give you a little advice.

Next time you are given a job, stretch it out."

"Okay, Phil, thank you."

I picked up my little, very little, check from the office and spent years evaluating Phil's words--stretch it out. You'd think a person would heed the lesson of the cigar factory experience and spend a lifetime stretching it out, milking it, sloughing off, but that wasn't what actually happened. I am simply unable to stretch it out. I have found that I do the job quickly, most times doing two, three or more things at once, getting the job done even before the expected due date and then begin on something quite new. I have expectations of myself. Thanks, Phil, wherever you are, but no thanks.

The next day I was sent on another job. I still needed to work, so I applied for and received a job in the wrapping department of a well-known well-respected, since-merged department store. It was nearing Christmas, and the wrapping department became the bustling energetic hub of the store. I was a lousy package wrapper. I couldn't follow all of their directions and added where I thought something should be added, plus my corners were not smooth--they bumped out--and the paper seams never matched. This was not acceptable in such a distinguished establishment. My manager liked me quite well; I considered it a kindness when she told me the jewelry department had an open position and she thought I would be perfect for the job. She was right.

Remembering the experiences with the cigar factory and the department store in Los Angeles reminded me of the job I had in high school working for an aunt of ours who had a costume jewelry, gift and pen store on Haight. The cousins and Marilynn wanted to work there, but Auntie said she thought I had the knack and the look. I worked for Auntie and Uncle throughout high school. My first sale was thrilling. The gentleman bought the whole set. He decided to buy the necklace, the earrings and the bracelet as well. I took his money and went to the cash register to ring it up. I put his money in the register and counted back nearly all of his money. I just took off the 64 cents and proceeded to count back his change.

As soon as I realized what I had done, I became faint and nauseous. I was brave enough to tell Auntie, "I just counted all of the money back to the man, and he didn't even tell me. I can't work here anymore because

I am so stupid."

"You are now my best salesperson and my best money person. You will never do that again, and it was a good lesson. Don't worry about it because I'm not worried, not one bit."

All the time I worked for Auntie and Uncle, Fields would be waiting for me at break time. When it was time to walk home, Fields would be there. We would have so much to say to each other, even if it had been only a few hours since we had seen and talked with each other. Fields loved me. I loved him. It was the kind of love that if you had a booger hanging out of your nose or a giant piece of lunch between your teeth, you were loved. There were no conditions, there were no demands to be made, no strain, no anxieties, and just being there was heaven for us. I have spent the rest of my life looking for this kind of love and have never found it again. I am thankful for knowing Fields. What if I would have never known that kind of love? I would have missed a faultless and complete corner of the love condition. I would have missed paradise on this earth. I had grown to trust Fields, and he and I had loved so dearly. We were experts in sucking air from one another's lungs.

We spent hours exploring our bodies, together and apart. I learned the subtleties of his body and how it fit into my own. He touched, smoothed and ran his fingers in and out of every pleasure part. Our bodies have felt the air passing between open parts, felt the smoothness of entry and the pang of powerful stirrings. Inside the walls the glide of a descending organ, only to be withdrawn and then descending over and over again until the moment has spent itself in a cascading warmth, exiting and entering, each feeling the warm wetness. We would rest and then begin again more slowly, more tactilely aware of entry being the beginning of the unutterable pleasure inside the middle of our existence. Eventually, the breathless pounding of our insides would ease into a quiet resting, and we would be aware of the swelling subsiding as our eyes and our smiles revealed our secret.

I know the reality of what I am saying. He and I would have grown apart as the years passed. I would have moved and married. He would have moved and married. We both would have had separate families, and at some unexpected reunion we would have seen how far apart we had grown. He would now look as old and as wrinkled as I do. Oh, but he would still be Fields. Fields will always be twenty-five and I will go on.   I still hear your voice. I still see you. You are not gone, but just resting somewhere waiting for me. Are you waiting for me, Fields? Are you waiting for all of us?

By mid-August, I was still working the jewelry counter at the well-known establishment within walking distance of Marilynn's apartment. When my teaching position came through, I became a part-timer. I never got over my fear of the cash register. Every time I had to approach it, I thought I was going to be gobbled up by a monster.

Painful Lessons

■■■ ■■

"THE GOOD LESSONS COME HARD AND COST DEAR."

Attending the university was a psychic pain for me that still gives me goose bumps and nightmares about final exams and not being able to find the right room, missing the exam and arriving on the wrong date, professors' voices reverberating day and night, fierce fears of unknown origins, and a lifelong case of irritable bowel syndrome. I finally devised a way to wear bobby socks with my Mary Jane's. That eased the foot pain, and the blisters finally healed. The nightmares have eased, but even now though over fifty years have passed, the gut aches still come with stress along with the insecurities of living one's life.

I was always spacing out in classes, but not with Dr. Bone. He captured my imagination and made the printed words soar above all else. I can hear him now standing in front of the roomful of students: "Class, you did not come here today to be entertained, I hope. You came to be enthralled with literature, I hope. You came to learn the language of the narrators and the protagonists. You came to learn about the creation of characters that mirror yourselves, I hope.

In any case, you're going to hear this story my friend Edward Albee told me when we were discussing his most recent success on Broadway. He said, 'The critics made such a big deal over the symbolism regarding a broom left casually leaning on the wall in the dining room. They wrote about ways that I had cleverly left the broom on stage throughout the play so that it alone added dimension and meaning to the characterization and the story line. They said that the broom symbolized the sweeping clean of the slate between the two main characters. They read into the broom all kinds of meanings I wish I had thought of myself. I did not have the heart to tell the media that the night man who sweeps and cleans the theater for the next day left the broom there and since it had so much symbolism attached to it and it meant so much to critics, I just decided to leave it there for the duration of the play.'"

Dr. Bone became an icon for many of us. He was someone who was uncritically admired, a symbol representing something we all came to the university seeking, each on a sliding scale according to our needs. Many of us came to his classes to gain knowledge, enlightenment, a road to travel and a means to get there. He made literature reign in an important and permanent place in our hearts and helped us to view it as an artistic endeavor.

I played around too much the first semester in college and took some extra time for an adjustment to academia. It was the first time I had been so far away from Fields. There were so many new and fresh ideas, so many new experiences. Through it all, Fields was my superman. I remember one evening as clearly as if it happened today. We had a sorority and fraternity exchange. I lived in the sorority house, so I just had to go downstairs or I most probably would not have attended this social. My mother's main aim in life was to have me attend this university and belong to this sorority. She worked for months getting me ready for rushing. She even had suits and dresses hand made by an expert seamstress who, while she spoke English, had a stiff accent from somewhere unrecognizable. The suits had little tucks and hand stitching.

The sorority/fraternity exchange was a yearly thing and happened around the homecoming game. Fraternities and sororities got together to get to know one another. You stood around, something like at high school dances, and waited for someone to ask you to dance. There, in my periphery vision, I saw a considerably good-looking, energetic fellow, bouncing around asking girls to dance. He was laughing and having a better time than the rest of us. I noticed that all of the girls he motioned onto the floor were shy and refused his beckoning by dropping their heads and shaking them. I thought to myself, if he asks me, I am going to dance no matter if I fall on my face.

As he made the rounds, I was somewhere in the middle. He eventually asked me. I accommodated him, knowing everyone was watching. I danced like I had always done in front of the cracked mirror on my bedroom closet door. His name was Buddy, great dancer, and he thought I was cool. Later, I found out he was the head cheerleader at our university. I didn't know that until I sat with my sorority sisters and watched with my surprised mouth hanging open during the homecoming half-time activities the next day. There was Buddy, out in front leading the cheers, megaphone in hand.

For years, Buddy and I were sometime friends. His great love and the number one lady in his life, Charlotte, was upstate, and he was faithfully waiting for her. He loved her with diligence, patience and pure devotion. Still, he wanted our friendship. He felt safe with me and knew that no more than a thoughtful, friendly friendship would be in our future. He knew about Fields.

I, as well, waited with diligence, patience and devotion until the next time Fields and I would see each other. Buddy married Charlotte but soon passed to the other side early in his life. Fields passed to the other side early in his life. Both men died too early. It isn't fair.

I sometimes wonder what Fields would look like now. I imagine him in different ways. I see an old crusty, crotchety man wrinkled and puffy. I see a handsome man who is aging gracefully, buff and fit with a ready smile for everyone. I see a grouchy, grumpy old fart that is annoyed by everyone and everything. I see an old man and an old woman dancing in the moonlight, kissing, stroking and loving. I see two people, a man and a woman sitting side by side in a home for the aging with heads bobbing up and down, wheelchairs locked together. I want to see nothing.

Fields was studying to be an architect and I was working on becoming a teacher. He was in one state and I was in a neighboring one. I was in San Francisco and Fields was in Portland. It was a day's drive, but there was a beeline highway between the two universities. We made many trips up and down that highway. The very first time I drove the beeline, I felt very grown up. I was flying along, brave and carefree, when the car stopped dead. What happened? I was horrified that I was out on this deserted road alone with a dead car. I was lucky. A family stopped, and the daddy diagnosed that I had simply run out of gas. I was supposed to be smarter than this running out of gas thing. Soon, luckily enough, I was on the road again. I ask, do you think I have ever run out of gas again? Right.

Another time I was bee lining it to Fields' university, a police officer stopped me on the road and had me get out of the car to walk the line. He looked me up and down, and up and down again. He said, "What are you, a beatnik or a bohemian?"

So very politely I answered, "Neither, I just like to wear long black stockings and gypsy skirts. I am a college student."

"Well, young lady, you should slow it down from here on."

"Yes, sir."

"You got a phone number I can call?"

"I have a steady boyfriend–we're going to get married."

"Alright."

Another time on that beeline trip, I got rear-ended and landed in a hospital in a very small town. That was the time the handsome, devoted-to-Charlotte cheerleader came to visit me and got me out of there. I want to say that this was the only time he ever did anything nice and or unselfish for me. Did I mention that throughout our friendship, it was hard not to notice his self-centered, self-serving ways?

Our friendship ended when we were both stuck at the same party one evening. Somehow, his buddies took his car and we ended up being the only two people left at this party with no ride home. He was determined to do something naughty, but I told him no! He got mad and proceeded with all of his male might. He said that I had to do what he said because I owed it to him. What a creep he turned out to be. There were a few little things left to eat, and after many hours of trying to get rides home, we were famished. He took all of the food and went into a corner and ate every bit of it by himself. That was it. I never spoke to him alone again. I mention Buddy here because he was good for my self worth. It was nice to be seen with the most popular guy on campus. In hindsight, the price I had to pay wasn't worth it.

Conversations With Sunshine
■■■ ■■

*"BETTER TO SHOOT OFF YOUR RIFLE BY MISTAKE THAN
YOUR MOUTH ON PURPOSE."*

The university days were coming to an end. All of
the requirements needed were being calculated and collected. The certificate to be recorded with the state for
my teaching credential said I was one credit short in a
foreign language. If the truth were known, I'm not very
good at languages, but after all of the classes and credits I
had accrued over the years, now lacking just one credit in
a foreign language was obscene. I decided to bolster up
my courage and talk to someone in an elevated position at
the university. I made an appointment with Dr. Bone, the

Dean of Education. I arrived a few minutes early. After waiting for forty minutes, I was allowed inside. Dr. Bone was a larger man than I remembered. He took up the entire seat behind the desk, and he could have put a few more inches to good use.

He was not a young man, nor was he old. He looked like my dad, stocky, strong and stern. He motioned for me to sit down in front of his desk. He was smack in the middle of having his lunch. Unwrapped sandwiches lay perpendicular to my seat, crackers and some cheese tidbits were positioned on the crumpled brown bag; he was sucking liquid from an old teacup and had the remains of mayo running down his chin.

Dr. Bone nodded at me and said, "Hope you don't mind me eating, but this is my lunchtime. You have a problem and I want to help you out here."

I explained my situation, and he nodded up and down. He seemed totally into what I was saying. His eyes were fixed on me even though his hands and mouth were having lunch. "Do you know anything about the waiver petition program?" he asked between nibbles of cheese.

"No I sure don't, sir."

"It's as easy as pie and if you get approved, which I think you will, you can go on with your life and your career. It's really quite simple. You get a waiver application from my secretary, fill it out, turn it in and wait."

I came across this waiver in an old jewelry box just recently. I held the box in the air and opened it slowly, expecting something to pop out. I remembered something special was inside that was as valuable as gold and diamonds. I guess that is why I put that waiver in the jewelry box along with gold and precious gemstones. This small blue rectangular paper states that it is an answer to a petition. Then it states that the action taken on the petition is shown on the reverse side. The other side of the paper says this petition is to satisfy the foreign language requirement for high school Spanish (12) and Italian (1) is approved. Gold and diamonds, rubies and pearls, and I could now go on with my life.

I began my first teaching position at Hancock Park Elementary School. One day I had an opportunity to pass by Dr. Bone's office. He had been transferred to the University of California at Los Angeles, and several classes from my school were touring the sculpture garden. I had noticed his name on a department roster posted on the door of the Department of Education as we passed.

I slipped away, leaving the children in the hands of the other teachers and the docent. I walked slowly, smiling to myself, happy to once again see Dr. Bone. It was lunchtime, and he was having lunch at his desk once again. I peaked through his office door, which was ajar, and told him that his advice about the waiver petition was an important part of what I was doing. I told him my class was outside touring the sculpture garden.

He acted like he remembered me, as if it were yesterday. He was full of more advice for me. He told me to have my students read five and six times a day no matter what the curriculum dictated. He said to assign them writing projects and make them write some more. He told me that math was a handy little skill but that it was not preeminent to all that future generations face.

Dr. Bertrand Bone prided himself on the fact that he did not even know all of his times tables and had to carry his ten fingers into the bank with him to make certain his deposits were correct. He recounted the times he won the estimation contests at his elementary school.

One time the corner drugstore had a contest to see who could guess how many gumballs were in a large container. Little Bertrand made certain that on the day they were to count the gumballs, he rose early and was the first one at the door when Mr. Copeland, the druggist and contest manager, arrived to open for business. Two hours later, the winner was announced. It was little Bertrand Bone. This was the first of many, many estimation triumphs. He estimated and won the marble count, the cotton balls, the ball bearings, and nickels in the fish tank. He was so good at estimation that he was finally disqualified to participate.

"Now", said Dr. Bone, "being disqualified for a talent, a skill or just plain being too good for something is quite a distinction and an accomplishment. Most people would have viewed being disqualified as a negative, but I just thought it was wonderful that I was so good at something no one else I knew could do."

I finally looked at my watch and said, "I hope to see you again, someday."

I hurriedly left Dr. Bone and joined the classes as they were ending their tour. It was lunchtime for everyone, but I wasn't hungry. I had just watched Dr. Bone devour his lunch with such gusto. In between bites, he fed me his philosophy, and I felt as if I had eaten every bite with him. His food was my food. For years, thereafter, my students read five and six times a day, and they wrote, wrote and wrote some more. Many of them are teachers themselves, producing strong readers and writers. Now, let me tell you that about 85% of all the students I ever taught can estimate to perfection. Do they know times tables, and do they have to take their fingers into the bank? Ask them.

Fields did not know his times tables and was never embarrassed about it. He used to say that he could figure out any problem using his fingers and a bunch of marbles. How did he become such an inventive architect if he couldn't multiply? He said multiplying had only to do with adding and he showed me. He lined up rocks and kicked each one out of the way as he counted, leaving a marker each time he kicked a ninth one. Soon he had seven counters of nine. He made a line of counters and then added them up.

"Nine markers of seven are sixty-three, okay, that

adding is done." We laughed, and I will never forget how sure he was of himself in adding and counting. He said that subtracting was taking things away and he wanted to do away with subtraction altogether. He thought subtracting was a negative concept and that dividing was not part of his vocabulary. He said that when you divide, somehow you subtract the multiplication and end up deficient.

I told a student about Fields and his math ideas when it came to my attention that the student counted on his fingers. I asked him if he wanted to take his fingers into the bank with him and, if he did, he would have to hide them under the counter. He said as long as he got his Mercedes, he didn't care.

Not long after I retired, the same student, who I had worried would have to take his fingers into the bank, called to tell me that his Mercedes was parked in his driveway and that his fingers worked very well. He asked me if I remembered saying that ain't wasn't in the dictionary and, until it was put in there, he couldn't use it. I said, "Yes, I remember saying that."

"Miss Epstein, I have a new dictionary and I looked up ain't and it is there, so I ain't worried about no times tables, I ain't worried about usin' my fingers and I ain't worried about nothing 'cause IT is parked in my driveway with the Mercedes circle on the hood and it ain't nobody's but mine." His American dream came true, and I ain't gonna mess with it.

At Opposite Ends

*"ALWAYS TRYING TO BE PERFECT CAN RUIN A
PERFECTLY GOOD LIFE."*

Marilynn and I spent lots of time together exploring the Southern California coastline. We should have invested every penny we had in real estate along the coast, but we all say that these days. We were so innocent of so many things.

We would put on our bathing suits, grab our towels--sun block had not been invented yet--and made our way to the beach. We compared our bodies each knowing but now strongly realizing the stark differences. Even though the same blood flowed through our veins, we were as dissimilar as two people from opposite ends of the earth. She was blonde and I was a brunette. She was thin like a rail and I was chunky. She had no boobs and I had enough for both of us; she called me Cow Tits and I called her Fried Eggs with Broken-Yolk. She was hazy in her thinking and I was crisp. She was farsighted and I was myopic. Her glasses magnified her eyes and mine turned my eyes into pinpoints. She looked at the material side of life and I looked to the spiritual. She liked her food mushy and hardly cooked, and I liked mine burned beyond recognition. She was impractical, and I was sensible and realistic. She always tried to make trouble for friends and relatives, and I always tried to keep the peace.

These differences took our lives in completely separate directions. Marilynn married twice and divorced twice. She had a daughter who married and divorced and is off on her own path. One thing true about Marilynn is that she worked all of her life. She was diligent and dependable on the job. Marilynn was the head assistant in an ophthalmology practice that was world renown in the diagnosing and the treatment of eye diseases and conditions. She had many aging patients who thought she was the illumination of their day.

I looked at the practical workable side of my life. She looked endlessly for something elusive.

We drove along the coast in Marilynn's convertible. We were full of giggles and laughter, accepting the whistles and hoots as an elixir from heaven. We were naïve, putting one foot in front of the other. We didn't know the first thing about the life here, but we entered with great enthusiasm and a prospect of hope and expectation. What did we expect? What was our hope? We hoped to meet the quintessential man of our dreams. We expected and hoped for the man who would carry us to our appointed destination--a man who would erase all of our tears and fears; a man who would ease our angst about our futures and ourselves; a man who would embellish and enhance our lives. We did not know that all other young women were looking into the same sunrises and sunsets and they wanted the same man for themselves. Born into our consciousness was competition. Who were we anyhow? How would we look up against a canvass containing millions and millions of others looking for the same conditions and connections?

Good Bye Marilynn

■■□ ■■

*"IF YOU THINK YOU ARE A PERSON OF SOME INFLUENCE,
TRY ORDERING SOMEBODY ELSE'S DOG AROUND."*

After I moved to Los Angeles, Marilynn stayed for several years, not loving it at all. She said it was a classless, uncultured wasteland. She said the weather caused the inhabitants to be inadequately dressed most of the year. Father had not let us come to the table unless we were fully dressed for all meals. Fully dressed meant that arms and legs were covered and necklines rounded. He always wore suits with rich-looking fabrics and specially tailored shirts; his ties and shoes were made in Italy. His hats were legendary. I have some of his hats in the back of my closet encased in a bundle of mothballs and cedar chips. Still the moths have had their way with Dad's distinguished and notable hats.

Mother wore clothes with the finest imported fabrics, gloves--always gloves--hats, and shoes extraordinaire. Her hats grace the back of my closet next to Dad's in their now-antique hatboxes. I pulled them out occasionally when the grandchildren were little, and we would play dress-up with Great-grandma's hats.

Marilynn and I had discussions about how weather conditions in San Francisco and all points north allowed for all that dressing. In Los Angeles, the days were warm most of the year, so folks shed their hats, gloves, and hardy clothing in exchange for simpler, lighter, airier, more comfortable dressing habits.

Showing your arms, neck and legs made for uncultured people, according to Marilynn. She was like our mother, who always had Emily Post's *Guide to Refinement and Culture* under her arm. We were taught at early ages to set an elegant table and use the colors of fruit and vegetables to make a dynamic presentation. Tomatoes were Mother's favorite. She accented places on her table with tomatoes of all sizes. She decorated with fruits and vegetables. She put drama into towers of vitals.

A small index card file sits on my dresser with all of Mother's favorite recipes in it neatly alphabetized. I have stared at that closed box for years. I think it is time to open the box and try my hand at making those crispy, rich chocolate brownies that were magnificent each time she made them, never over- or under-cooked, never cut in different shapes, always squares--or maybe those perfectly baked chocolate chip cookies, that lovely and delicately seasoned tamale pie, or her mandel bread. Her crepes were renowned, her lemon pound cake melted in your mouth; her Hawaiian meat balls were loved by all, copied by all, but no one ever got them quite right. Her baked chicken with secret sauce is missing from this box, her special spinach dish that disguises spinach so you don't know what you're eating is missing, too. I wonder if Marilynn took some of Mother's recipes? I wonder if she ever made any of them. I will never know.

When Marilynn moved back to S.F., she picked up in that city, the city of her birth and youth, just where she left off. Very soon after taking up residence in Mom and

Dad's house, she met a soldier in the U.S. Army, actually a Lieutenant, and spent some time in Paso Robles when he was stationed at Fort Ord. She played the Lieutenant's wife perfectly, or so it seemed to me. I chuckled to myself the first time I came to visit her and her Lieutenant. It was 112 degrees, worse heat and less culture than anywhere in Los Angeles. Marilynn was nearly shirtless and certainly had very little covering her legs. The apartment was hot and dry. Actually, it was stifling and rather miserable. Who could enforce a strict dress code and culture in that heat?

Marilynn was so much more talkative than I had ever known her to be. Sometimes she was downright hateful with the things she would say about her neighbors. She did make some friends, one in particular whose look reminded me of the early 60's Barbie Doll. The new friend's name was Roberta, and her husband was also a Lieutenant, working as a dentist. Marilynn's husband was a doctor. Both Roberta and Marilynn died youthful deaths; looking back, how could we have known their fates?

I remember visiting Marilynn in her own home in San Francisco eventually, which sat so close to the ocean the wind would come off the water and blow colder than Pluto. Her home was filled with antiques she had gathered from relatives long gone. She had a mirror that I looked into and saw my grandmother's reflection. Perhaps it was my own reflection, mirroring my grandmother's. The cushions on the down sofas in the living room puffed up so high that when you sat down, it took awhile for the air to escape and for you to settle into a seat level with your weight.

Marilynn had framed pictures of everyone in the family that recorded their gradient rises, successes, age and beauty. Everyone in our family was beautiful in some way or another. This is, of course, an opinion of someone who loved them all. The photos caused comments and discussions each time anyone from the family came to visit. We all were certain to send her our latest photographs, knowing that she would frame them and they would be on display for our next visit.

It took Marilynn only a few years after returning to San Francisco to seem to know everyone, and everyone seemed to know her. She knew the best bakeries and butchers, where to get the best steak sandwich or floral arrangements–which she had delivered every week. She knew the best seamstress, cleaners, cleaning lady, window cleaners, painters and any other services you needed; they were her best friends. She was a strong member of her community. She worked especially hard to make the schools better by serving on the school board as a member at large.

The last time I spoke to Marilynn was over 40 years ago. I am not certain why she stopped speaking to me, but she did. She thought I did something to offend her, but that something she thought I did lies with her in her burial site because it is not known to any of us. Cancer is what got her; cancer is what got all of our grandmothers and grandfathers, and their ancestors. I feel like I am waiting in line for my turn. I just hope that I do not get to the head of the line too quickly.

Marilynn died too young to get some of the other diseases that awaited her. She wasn't old enough to have to deal with glaucoma or cataracts. Her body didn't have enough time to develop heart disease, kidney failure, or any of those autoimmune diseases. She just contracted cancer before any of the others could take hold. In some ways she left this earth without having to stand in line very long.

Marilynn, I want you to know, posthumously, how much you helped in your innocent way to build my self-esteem. You didn't know it, but by your very nature, you made me stronger. Everything I did, you copied. You didn't know you copied me, but you did. When I made ribbon woven pillows, you made them, too. When I collected porcelain shoes, you collected them, too. Actually, your shoe collection far surpassed my own and was donated to a museum in San Francisco that promised to display your collection for years to come. When I began to grow Bonsai trees, you did, too. When I began to knit, you knitted. I must admit you knitted much more productively and expertly. Over the years I have come to realize that you respected me much more than you would have ever admitted. Thank you, Marilynn, and good-bye. May you rest in peace. You were not able to say good-bye to me, so good-bye to you.

Days Of Fields

■■■ ■■

"THERE ARE MANY TRAILS TO THE TRUTH, BUT NO SHORTCUTS."

Fields would have saved me from this life of look-ing--a life of desperation, of longing, with an ache and a yearning I had not ever imagined was part of the human saga. He was not big around, but he was long. When we lay together on the lawn in the park, his legs would ex-tend far beyond my own. I don't think we ever discussed bodies or how they looked, fit together, were a match, or whether we liked each other or ourselves. That was not part of who we were.

We would lie on the grassy knoll within sight of the

Palace of Fine Arts and count the stars. Our bodies would blend, obscuring where one began or the other ended. We just floated together while our surroundings stayed at ground level. We never worried that we would not blend. It had been happening ever since we began lying down together, and we did not question it because it was our way of being–floating. I never floated with anyone before Fields and I never have again since he's been gone. Eugenia so much wanted to be part of our inner lives, but she could not.

Brock, Fields' brother, entered my life momentarily after Fields departed. We thought we could replace Fields with each other. We did not succeed even for a moment. I wanted something of Fields, but not of Brock. There are times today when I think I see Fields running towards me, his hair stroked over to the left, his eyes gleaming, his arms outstretched, his mouth open in expectation, his hands catching the wind--and then he passes.

Brock died a few years after I moved to Los Angeles. He was serving in the Marines when Fields died and was sent overseas. He returned safely, applied for a job in South Carolina, went there for an interview and became quite ill. He was hospitalized and several weeks later died of peritonitis.

Eugenia called to tell me; immediately my heart went out to her, but mainly to their mother. She had lost both her sons. Unimaginable, but it happened to her. It has happened to others. I asked Eugenia how her mother was doing, and she said it had changed her in ways she would have a hard time explaining.

She did share several things with me. Her mother's voice had gone down several octaves, and she sounded like a man. Eugenia also said that her mother's hair had fallen out in large patches, leaving bald spots that were hard to hide. How could anyone hide the loss of one son, now two? Her voice, her hair, those were outside manifestations; I can't begin to imagine what happened to her inside. Eugenia felt her own loss but didn't give it voice.

A multitude of years have meandered around the bend in the river, but the events still peal loudly in some hearts and judgments. Fields and I had been together, connected at our hipbones, for some time. Actually, the events I am about to relate happened during the middle years of our relationship. I was very friendly with Fields' mother, and his sister and brother. I spent many comfortable days in the home of the Fields family. My mother was as far as I could tell about friendships between mothers, a best friend with Fields' mother. I was blind-sided by the events that followed.

The Mom, I always called her The Mom, went to church, Our Lady of Grace, with her three kids in tow every Sunday. By now you could hardly call the three tall, well-structured young adults following "The Mom" into the church, kids, but she always called to them, "Come on, kids."

This crisp, Sunday morning, The Mom surprised everyone who was within range by lying down at the church entrance, arms and legs outstretched, and screaming in a high-pitched voice, "My son is next to a Jewess. He is breaking with our rules. He is near the Jews. Lord, help my son to break away from that filth and our tragedy. Make the Jewess give him back to me." I heard about this event, not from Fields, but from an auntie in their family. She told me so I would give Fields back to them. I tried to calm myself down so I could explain some things to this auntie, but I could only shake my head.

In the next few days Fields apologized and said he didn't want me to ever know about the explosion his mother had on the steps leading to church, but by then I had done my homework. I learned that a Jewess is a Jewish girl or woman. Until then I had no idea that Fields' mother was so unhappy about our camaraderie. I didn't know she held my presence in such disdain. I am glad I did not know it then and am remorseful I know it now.

Several days after the screaming fit, I told my grandmother what happened that day on the steps of Our Lady of Grace. She said, "Dear, I just don't understand it."

I said, "I understand it. She hates me because I'm a Jewess."

"Now, now," she said. "Do you know that Fields' dad is Jewish?"

"What?"

My grandmother was a strong conversationalist, but when you needed to know something in a hurry, she rushed her words together and it seemed like she got the entire sentence out in one long word.

"Fields' mother and father were sweethearts all through high school, and only through a long, long conversion were they able to marry in the church."

"Did you go to the wedding, grandma?"

"No, but your mom and dad went"

"They did? What did they say?"

"Your mom came home and told me that the priest told the whole congregation that the issue from that marriage would never be Jewish, so that there was no question that the children would be raised Catholic."

"Well, I'll never tell Fields unless he mentions it to me." I made a promise to myself that day.

"He doesn't know, and my guess is he won't ever know unless you tell him."

"I won't tell him," I said.

This bit of the Fields family history was tucked under the rug like unwanted dust. A few people knew, but like many things it was forever unspoken. I wanted to shout my news to the moon. I wanted to tell Fields and we would live quietly but not innocently under the stars. It never happened and I never told. The Mom, Fields' mom, had always suffered bouts of suicidal depression, a genetic thing, and before this, I had felt the need from time to time to be there for her. Little did I know that a

Jewess so close to her, or her precious son, at any time, could be of no comfort at all.

It is true, Fields' dad was missing for most of his childhood, and the details were scant. Fields knew his father's name was Martin and that he looked just like his father. A spitting image, some people in the neighborhood would say. There was no doubt in Fields' mind that his dad was run out of their home for some reason. He remembered harsh words being bantered back and forth between his mom and dad, but he couldn't remember the words or their meanings.

The Mom kept the family wrapped tightly in the secrets and mysteries of Catholicism. Fields was wrapped tighter than anyone. One day, the wrapper burst open, and Fields said it felt like he was a newly hatched baby chick, all soft, fragile and ready to grow. He grew away from the church and all of its teachings, except he always knew that there was a force guiding his way and that when his life was finished he would ascend to his proper place. He told me that he had learned enough during his wrapped years that he would always be devoted to his origins. What had happened to his dad, he might never know, but I vowed I would try to find out. I longed to be able to tell him.

Fields is buried in St. Mary's Cemetery in Oakland. When I was younger, I traveled back many times to the gravesite that held my Fields. I told him so many things. I knew he was there each time because there was a familiar touch and a blowing of the wind. The last time I sat near his grave, I looked out to see if the trees were blowing in the wind, but they were perfectly still. The wind was only blowing in the spot where I stood, blowing over me, telling me things.

Preparations had been made for Fields and his confirmation day. He was assigned the task of choosing his saint. After studying and deliberating about many saints, he chose St. Nicholas, also known as Father Christmas, because he loved to give gifts. It is said that St. Nicholas saved the fate of a friend's three daughters by throwing bags of gold in their windows for a dowry. Since Fields' birth date is December 6th, it seemed an obvious choice. In the earliest of religious traditions, saints are remembered by the date of their passing from this life to the spiritual side. Fields was born and died on December 6th, the feast day of St. Nicholas. After my first child was born,

miraculously on December 6th, I knew it was time to journey back to see Fields. I traveled alone because there was
not a single soul to share my memories, or at least that is
what I thought.

I arrived at the spot where Fields lies four years
to the day when he took his last breath, not in my arms,
which I regret and am still trying to avenge the wrong. As
I stood on the spot where I hoped the recognizable winds
would blow, I realized that Fields was at peace with his two
halves, both the Hebrew and the Catholic half. He had
become whole. He had lived and died to become worthy
of love and devotion.

Field's official confirmation in the church never
took place. I do not know why the anointment, the blessings, and the reaffirmations did not happen, but I know
Fields felt their power and shed them on those who loved
him. He didn't need to be anointed by the church; he had
his own way of achieving blessings. He told me that he
felt blessed by his heavenly father many times a day. He
told me that he was able to share his blessings through the
blowing of the wind. Feel Fields' wind.

As I sat on the spot where Fields lies, memories of

my own confirmation flooded my memory. I was called to the Rabbi's office. This was something different. I was well behaved and was a good tutor for the rest of the girls when they needed a push along the path to our confirmation. The temple only had a Bar Mitzvah for the boys. The girls had a confirmation. We were to be the second confirmation class. All of us were just turning thirteen.

We studied in an upstairs room of the temple and we were all happy to be there studying for our confirmation. We were best friends, and every Tuesday, Thursday and Sunday, we would bounce up the stairs, anxious to hear from all of our friends. We were in a time of our lives of pure trust, pure love, and innocence. We had little acceptance in our outside lives, but inside those hallowed walls we were one with ourselves.

Our temple was not an orthodox temple but held to many of their rigid rules. Women and children were delegated to the upstairs, and they did not even think of wandering to the ground level. We did have to enter the temple on the ground level and once upstairs descend to ground level to use the restrooms, we helped in the kitchen which was on the ground level, but we never enjoyed the full breadth of the lower levels. I remember a time when the Rabbi relaxed some rules for a fashion show, but this was many years later. I will return to the fashion show.

I dawdled getting to the Rabbi's office. He was busy with someone else, so I waited. I was nervous and knew something was going to happen. I picked at my nails and scratched at my elbows; the tic in my face went on a rampage. He finally turned his attention to me and paused for what seemed like hours. I could tell he was composing his thoughts, organizing what and how he was going to say what he said. His brows closed together, he started a low groan, and I began to sweat. My mouth went dry, my glasses fogged and my heart began to beat rapidly in anticipation. The Rabbi looked at me with such distance, such conviction. He said in his very thick accent, "Well, Sunshine, you will not be confirmed with the rest of the girls."

"What? Why not? What happened?"

"It is my decision that the cut-off date for confirmation girls is August 31st, and your birthday is September 19th. That means you are not eligible."

"But Rabbi, I can speak and write Hebrew better than all of them. I help them. You can't leave me out of the group."

"I can, I just did and you will have to come back for another year. You will be confirmed next year."

It felt like bomb exploded inside of me. All of the venom I had felt brewing, boiling, fermenting, in me spewed out in a blast. "God damn you, Rabbi, shit on you. I will never come back into your temple again. I hate you. I hate this temple."

I ran from that temple and ran all the way home with tears running and heart breaking. All the way home, I was talking with God, asking questions I wanted answered, answering them myself, screaming out obscenities, not really meaning any of it, but feeling quite powerful by the time I reached home. My parents were pillars in the temple, and I knew I had some pretty big explaining to do. I knew the Rabbi would spill all that I had said and give my parents an earful of their obscene daughter's mouth and her unladylike manners. I didn't care by then, because I was never going back into that temple, but I also knew that I would be the best Jewish person I could be on my own.

I know that everything I have ever learned I have learned on my own. Oh, certainly there have been guides, many of them along the way, but it took perseverance and the will to learn to make an intellectual life happen.

After all of our children were born, I knew I would have to preserve in them the culture and give them a respect for Judaism. If I really meant what I said about never going back into the temple, I would have to work hard to give them knowledge and the history of the Jewish people. I taught it to them the way it was taught to me. As the years passed, I made big parties at holiday times, and I made the stories powerful to insure permanence in the psyche of each of our children. I did not know then, that leaving the temple and never returning meant that I would always have to be on a waiting list. I know about waiting lists. I have always been on one in one way or another. I found out early that my family had genetic disorders and diseases. I have always known that I was in line or on a waiting list for something. Now, this was the time for my third letter to God.

"Dear God, I am in line and please do not make the line move too quickly. I am on the waiting list, but I do not wish to cash in on it. Just let the line jam up and the list continue to be at a standstill. I do not wish to win. I do not wish to be first in line. I hate lines. Thanking you in advance for your time. Sincerely, Your eternal servant."

One year, the Rabbi asked my parents if he could come to my Seder table on the first night of Passover. This Passover event, where I spent ten days preparing for and many days receding from, is where I was to receive my confirmation as a Jewish person, my blessing and re-affirmation of the faith. Although I was never to return to the temple fold, I taught my family all that I knew and inspired some of them to go on and learn more.

This Rabbi, who had turned me away from my people, wished to make amends. He came bearing the *20 Haggadahs for the American Family*; two books by Max Dimont, *Jews, God And History* plus *the Indestructible Jews*; and some timely Jewish publications. He sat quietly and recited some prayers when asked. He seemed pleased to be with us for the ancient Hebrew ritual done in English by a little family in a spot on this earth that was ours. When our son asked why this night was different from all other nights, I wanted to say so much of what you now know, but smiled and let my husband answer the best he knew how.

Although Fields and I did not receive our confirmations in a holy blessed way among our respective parishioners, we both achieved our confirmations in our own way, in ways that gave us peace. We prayed, we gave and asked for forgiveness. We atoned for our errors in the physical sense and our errors in judgment. We helped ourselves to grow in the image of God and we sought ways to assist, support, and cooperate with others. We worked to achieve piety and mercy. We lived sincere and honest lives; we had love for God, our neighbors, truth and ourselves.

I am returning to the fashion show because I said I would. There are two pictures in my memory box that stand out from all other photos and papers. One is of the fashion show which was another confirmation for me. I still look into the faces of all of the girls and wonder where they are today. Did their confirmation that day mean as much to them as mine did at our Seder table that Passover so many years after I was scheduled for the formal one in the temple?

Also, there is a rather large professional fashion show

portrait of me. You should see how cute I was–that cute little thing Fields loved, adored, believed in. I thought all of the tall girls looked the best, but in this one photo, I looked the best. We all felt like models and it should have done a lot for our self-esteem. I don't know if that experience did it for them, but looking at this single photo, I see what Fields saw. I see me.

Lost And Won
■■■ ■■

"NOTHING THAT BAD OR THAT GOOD LASTS THAT LONG."

There was a time, an awful time, when Fields was lost to me. I knew where he was physically, but mentally and in love, I did not. There came rumors of his infatuation, a crush he had on a girl named Florenzia, also a senior in our high school, and in the same English and science classes. Her family lived on Buena Vista Avenue, the street that surrounds the park. Florenzia's family home was just four short blocks from the Fields' home. Her face had an indelible glow and her hair was legendary. Her hair extended in thick waves to her buttocks. It was the color of concord grapes drying in the sun and it turned up at the ends. It glimmered in the light of day and exuded a commanding luster in the evening lights. Her body was as smooth and soft as a ripe peach and it curved strongly in places where your hand would slide.

She didn't ask for anything except to look into your eyes and wait. There was never a time when she looked away or became distracted. She wasn't into herself, she was into others, and she was especially into Fields, into waiting for Fields. What she was waiting for I do not know, but Fields knew she was waiting for him. Florrie, as he called her, was the type of woman who let the man lead in every way. She loves Fields. She follows Fields.

Florrie's score was the highest on a special test given by the university for job placements. Actually, it was the highest performance to date by anyone. Fields noted in his diary that they went to someone's birthday party, and the guests played a game. It was one of those unscramble the words games with twenty-five scrambled words. Florrie correctly finished unscrambling those words in less than three minutes. Fields had four words done, only three correct, when the game ended. Fields wrote that Florrie was the smartest woman he had ever known, ever will know.

I had to accept whatever Fields was doing because he would do the same for me. It was a prerequisite for what was to come later. Something was wrong. I just didn't know what it was. I knew that I just had to let it be that way. I had to honor and love them both because by loving Fields, I loved Florrie.

Florrie took Fields into the Tao of the 60's–candles, crystals, gemstones, and energy from the earth, herbal healing, alternative and spiritual guides. He began to spout truths as they were revealed to him. Remember the *Be Here Now Guide* we all fell madly in love with, that big purple book that gave us the knowledge that your highest teacher is You, yourself. He spouted this philosophy of love, of being open and spiritually loving above all, curious and enthusiastic. It was a time people were striving for peace and love. To this day, tie-dyed clothing is still very much in style. What it represents is a freedom and the beauty of cosmic consciousness. In every tie-dyed shirt, I see the center of gravity and the universe revolving around it.

One day this last summer, my children and grandchildren gathered around the kitchen table, and we made tie-dyed shirts. It amazes me that they are as timely today as they were over forty-five years ago. While making the shirts, I told them about tying the knots and that the untying of the knots once the dyeing process has been completed is a symbol of untying the knots that bind you. Each shirt is unique and the excitement of untying is gratifying. The one that I made turned out to be a traditional bulls-eye pattern with a definite center and rings of color outwardly radiating.

We played music from the hippie subculture while we worked. The music of that era is poetic with the singing of dreams, wishes and experiences in the American culture. I love it and enjoy it today as much as I did back then. I think, though, that Fields and Florrie and I were not only products of the 60's, but the 50's, and perhaps the Beat Generation played an even stronger influence.

As one of my grandchildren untied her shirt, I was instantaneously brought back to the day when Fields wore a shirt nearly identical in its spiral pattern, with the light green and purple colors matching what this child gleefully held up for our inspection.

The day Fields wore the nearly identical shirt that my grandchild had just made, he told me about his observations of meetings he had been required to attend as part of setting up some building contracts. He identified a pecking order. Chickens peck from the top down. At each meeting the same chickens pecked first and then the rest followed. Since Fields was the newest member of the firm and thus last in the pecking order, he rarely spoke at these meetings. He was spoken to but not given any time to respond.

We learned about pecking order and had first-hand observations at my Uncle Donald's chicken farm in Petaluma. Uncle Donald brought Mama and his other sisters fresh eggs every week from the farm. He and Aunt Alice were expected every Sunday for dinner, and he would distribute the eggs. We didn't go to visit them often because they made their weekly trips to us, but on some occasions we had chances to go to the farm.

Fields and I would take the buses out to the country and visit Uncle Donald and Aunt Alice. They were wonderful to visit. Uncle Donald would walk you all over the territory. You would see not only his farm but also the farms of his neighbors. Aunt Alice would have freshly baked bread and farm butter ready for us to eat. If you are city folks and you have never had an opportunity to taste real farm butter, this is what happens. Your mouth melts to the consistency of the butter, and you know you have tasted something real, something that cannot be reproduced anywhere but there.

One time Aunt Alice made a fresh pound cake, of course, using farm butter. It tasted different than anything else I'd ever eaten. If I close my eyes today, I can still taste the rich denseness of a true natural thing. I can taste Fields.

Fields, as I called him, his friends and his family called him, was really Fletcher Fields, according to his birth certificate. He was very surprised to find out from one of the older architects in the firm in Seattle that had hired him, a man who took Fields under his wing, that there was a Fields family living in the area. The older architect said that Martin Fields was president of the country club.

One morning before the firm's weekly meeting, Fields' new friend said, "Fletch, you are the spitting image of this guy Martin. You ought to come to the club tonight and see for yourself. I can pick you up on my way over there." They called my darling Fields, Fletch at the firm. No one had previously called him Fletch or even Fletcher except his father.

"You sure this guy looks like me?"

"Spittin' image. You interested?"

"Yeah, I am. I'll think about going to the club with you sometime, but not tonight. I have somewhere I have to be."

Fletch Fields let weeks go by without taking up the invitation to go to the country club meeting He felt certain that he had found his father, but had to figure out some things and weigh the idea. He remembered that his family always said that he was the spitting image of his dad. He was intrigued, but if he passed on the offer to find out about his father, his life would continue on as it was, and he was happy with the way things were turning out for him. If he met and rekindled a relationship with his father, how would this meeting change things in his life?

He pondered what it would do to his thinking if he

did find his father and how it would affect his life if he
didn't meet this Martin Fields, perhaps his dad. There
must be hundreds of Martin Fields in the world, so why
this one? This was the one put in his path. Was this Martin
Fields, the one he was destined to have some link with, or
was this man a Martin Fields like the rest of the hundreds,
perhaps thousands, in the universe? If Fields were to meet
his father now after so many years, would he include his
mother and sister Eugenia? Would he meld the family of
the past with the present one?

Fields and I talked by phone about how he should
handle this new information. How could I tell Fields at that
point about what my grandmother had said about Fields'
father and how and why he left his family? "Religions constraints," my mother had said. How could I tell him he
was Jewish?

My mother and Fields' mother had spent hours
consummating their friendship when they lived right next
door. They would take walks through the parks on either
side of their community and they would talk. The Mom,
Fields' mom, would always hint at things. She often said
that Martin Fields was a mystery and many of the things

that he told her, she later found out were not the truth.

At one point, she said he was distant and had some mysterious dealings with men of our culture, meaning Jews. She was sure that he had a family he kept secret, but one time someone she didn't recognize knocked on the door. The man on her doorstep looked like he could have been Martin's brother because they were the same height and weight, with the same nose, eyes spread too far apart, beak mouth too small for such a big face, and ears that stood away from their heads readying them for take-off into full flight.

The Mom told my mother that when Martin heard about the man at the door, he became so unglued that he demanded that everyone in the family bundle up and go for one of their walks. He told Mrs. Fields not to come back for an hour. This is the day she met us and we all walked.

This is the day she told my mother that she found secret things in an old richly carved wooden box. She said they were things my mother would understand, and she asked my mother to come over and look at the things in the box. My mother, a small woman with bowed legs and a deep widow's peak, always ready with an open smile, went over to Mrs. Fields' home the next day and opened the box of secret things. With her head bent into the box, she was brought into this secret world that was not a secret to her.

She was overwhelmed, but calmed her racing heart and caught her breath before she explained that the two brass candles must have been from an older member of his family. My mother explained about the lighting of the Friday night candles ushering in the beauty of the Sabbath. She explained about the plain but strong-looking menorah. Mrs. Fields had seen lit menorahs in the windows of some neighbors.

The box also contained three prayer shawls, which my mother assumed belonged to members of Martin's unknown family. There, covered in a soft doily, was another carved box housing several pieces of gold and diamond jewelry. One was a diamond-spattered Star of David on a chain that still sparkled after so many years hidden in the box, and the other a gold and diamond mezuzah worn, by the look of the chain it was linked to, around the neck of a man of distinction. Most importantly, the bottom of the box housed a bundle of photos.

I sighed and put these memories away. I had promised myself that I would never tell Fields about his father being Jewish. It was not my place.

I wondered if I should counsel him to just let this Martin Fields sighting disappear into space, to disintegrate, to keep Fields separate and able to go on his way. But I knew that Fields would not let it happen that way. Fields had his own way to handle situations and to deliver, if only unto himself, a satisfactory answer. He needed to explore this man's identity, and he needed me to go on this journey with him. I needed to be there for him, with him. I sat in my assigned seat on the train heading north to Seattle.

The Long Train Ride
◻■◻■◼

"DON'T TRY ON ANOTHER MAN'S HAT. IT IS ALMOST AS BAD AS GETTING ON HIS HORSE."

So much time, so many sunrises and sunsets have come and gone, but still I know Fields best from the inside out. Florrie did not accompany Fields to Seattle. She had gone back to San Francisco to be with friends and family, promising to join him in Seattle as soon as he was settled. Many moons waxed and waned, but Florrie did not come. Fields said he knew that their work together was done when the last glimpse of her backside appeared to him as she boarded the bus going in the opposite direction his bus would take him. They might remain good friends.

Not necessarily best friends, but best friends for the spiritual and enlightening work they had done together.

She had enlightened Fields to the realization that he was in charge of his own destiny. She showed him he could pick and choose directions and pointed out that sometimes the road taken by the fewest may be his best route. Even if it turned out to be not the best route, it would at least be the least crowded.

Fields and I certainly hadn't picked a place less crowded when we decided to attend a prefab show and architecture conference at the Cow Palace. There were so many people crowded into one space that it felt like we could easily be trampled, so many people that it was hard to breathe. The next day I had bruises all up and down my right side. It was strange to be so one–sided, and I didn't even remember bumping into anything on that side. Fields said, after viewing the bruises, "Oh, you lead with your right." I did then and I still do.

I was going to Seattle to be with Fields. The crisis of Florrie not returning to him had passed. His job was going well, very well, and Fields and I had come to an understanding that, through both the substantial and the slim-pickings of times, we were bound and glued together forever. When Fields called to tell me he thought he found his father, the glue dried and our bindings grew tighter. I was going to be with Fields. I knew it was going to be a very long, interminable bus ride and terribly uncomfortable, so I elected to take the train. Still a long ride, but bearable, hopefully.

The train started its journey with a lurch, announcing its intent to move forward. Thank goodness I was seated. I put some of my things on the empty seat next to me, hoping that by nightfall I would have that seat available for me to stretch out for the long night's haul. I didn't know then about berths and dining cars.

As soon as the train was settled into the gentle moving rhythm, a small, young gentleman in a suit and tie, who was sitting across the aisle, caught my attention and began a conversation with me. He asked if I was planning to go to the dining car. His question didn't really register, but I nodded yes. He invited me to go with him, and again I nodded yes. He led the way, I followed and was treated to a long room lined on both sides with tables next to windows that let in sights passing almost before

you could register them. He motioned to a table halfway
through the car. We sat opposite each other, looking hesi-
tantly into faces we had never before seen.

He said, "Chas Littlewood."

"Sunshine Epstein"

He was soft-spoken, sort of sweet. He was beautiful
in the way his inner spirit shone through. He shared that
not only was he traveling for a textile company wanting to
make railroad ties in Portland, but he was hoping that riding the rails while on this journey would help him, as he was
looking for a deeper meaning to his life. He said that he
was always seeking the meaning of things, but could never
quite pin them down. He said that every once in a while
things seamlessly came together and pieces of the puzzle
fit for him, but sadly, he said, there were not enough of
those times. I told him I always believed that people were
put dead center so that you could recognize them as your
teacher. Oh, not one who scratches the chalk across the
board and yells at you when your eyes stray, but a teacher
of life--one who is there physically sometimes for only an
instant but remains forever in your memory.

"Okay, so, Sunshine, what is important to you?"

"My friends, I guess."

"What is so important about them?"

"They keep me floating."

"As opposed to drowning?"

"You could say that. What is important to you, Chas?"

"My friends."

We both laughed.

"What makes you happy, Sunshine?"

"An absence of pain."

"Me, too."

I had a BLT on lightly toasted bread. It was the tastiest sandwich I ever had. I munched silently, not realizing the world was around me; I was just into the taste, the creamy texture of the mayonnaise as it coated the way down to my stomach. I remember the sandwich was cut into four triangles, and when I finished one, I was so happy that I had three more to go. When I finished the third one and there was one still to be devoured, bliss. Whether it was the scenery, the chef or the company I do not know, but I have remembered that particular BLT, that particular train ride and that teacher all of my life

Chas and I finished the evening talking in the dining car. We were not attracted to each other in any way other than sharing time and talk. He told me of his girlfriend who was nearly a foot taller and how they would get stares and little mouth-covered chuckles when they were out in public.

He told me that when he left she was fretting over the fact that she had worn a hole in her slippers. They were her most important slippers; she said the hole meant they were wearing out and she couldn't stand the fact that she would have to give them up. She said they were so comfortable and no other slippers were as good. What was she going to do? He said that she was in such a state of worry that he had to call her mother to calm her down. He was out the door, leaving for the train station, and he left her with her fear of losing her most precious slippers.

He said that she had little breakdowns like this often. He recounted a time she had purchased two skirts. They were similar in color and style, but one was shorter and the other longer. She tried them on and took them off many times. She kept asking Chas which one he liked the best. Each time he would tell her, she would help him change his mind by showing him how they looked with the sweaters she had to go with them and how one was much more practical than the other. He finally told her to keep both of them and that would be the end of it, so he thought.

If she wasn't the most beautiful girl he had ever seen he would have been long gone before the skirt and slippers incidents. He would have been gone when she could not decide which bowl would house the Halloween candy, gone when she worried how much to spend on a wedding gift for a mutual friend, gone when she set and reset a table for four with different settings, cloths, centerpieces, chairs in and out of storage, menus and all for two extra people. He said he thinks she is crazy but loves her beauty.

I told him about Fields, about our lifelong relationship. I told him that we used to play as toddlers, and that we used to walk to Buena Vista Park and hike along the retaining walls. I told him that we could see bits and pieces of headstones from ancient times stuck into the walls. I told him we used to pretend we could see the ghosts of the people from the 1700's and 1800's because we pretended, or maybe we really saw them dressed in the clothes of that period. I remember a time when we felt hugged and embraced by cold, prickly hands and arms. They were the remains of someone long gone. Our hair was blowing and feathers were falling from the sky making a path to lead us to a quiet spot. Voices drifted in and out of range.

I told Chas how we went to the library and saw pictures of people dressed like the ghosts we saw at the park. We began to believe in ghosts. I told him how Fields broke with the church and how his mother had the family under some sort of a spell.

I told Chas that one evening years ago there was a special mass, and Fields thought it would be good for us to go together. I told him that I was looking for a sign from God to tell us that there really was something up there that we should love and care about. We parked my car, a '55 Chevrolet stick shift. I mention the stick shift for a reason. We sat through the mass from beginning to end. I prayed or performed what I thought to be prayer. I think I caught Fields praying as well. I asked for a sign. I prayed for a sign. I desperately needed a sign that there was something and someone up there to believe in forever.

Mass was over, and the people began to parade out of the doors into the parking lot. What had happened to my car? It was not where I parked it. Lots of cars were leaving the parking lot, causing some minor chaos and some confusion for us. We finally found my car, with the bumper and hood up against the light post. I remember I screamed, "My car rolled, oh my god, it rolled."

Fields said, "Now there is a sign from the heavens."

I prayed for a sign so that I could believe forever. I have never needed another sign, but they come nearly daily now. I think the signs were always there, and the reason I see them more often is that I am getting better at reading them. If my car had rolled into the main street, there could have been an accident, maybe a fatal one. That was my sign from the heavens. Fields said that I just didn't know how to handle a shift car and must have left it in neutral.

It was time for Chas and I to part. He said that by early morning we would be pulling into Portland and he would be on his way. We were both grateful for the conversations and the companionship. We smiled and parted. In that short amount of time I had grown to love Chas because he was a superior listener and a high-quality person. I was certain that we would never see each other again, but I was delighted with the moments of sharing on that train ride. He would find a deeper meaning for his life; he would just have to wait for it.

When I returned to my seat, the seat next to me was still empty. Thankfully, I spread out my coat, made a little place for my purse pillow and closed my eyes. I was astounded that the rhythm of the rails truly sounded like a Beethoven piano sonata I had partially learned when taking piano lessons with Mrs. Vans.

How did the piano lessons and Mrs. Vans enter my mind right then on that train ride that would take me to Fields? Why did the humiliation of those lessons plague my thoughts right then? How were Mrs. Vans and those lessons part of my journey? Would the thought of them help me to help Fields?

I thought I hated Mrs. Vans. I thought I hated piano lessons. I thought I hated music. In retrospect, I hated the disrespect. I hated having my fingers banged on the right notes, not taking into consideration I was a little girl with fragile fingers. At the end of each piano lesson, my mother would pick me up right on time. Mrs. Vans would smile as she accepted payment, and my mother would be unaware that my fingers were sprained and just short of being broken.

We had a pecan-colored Jonas Chickering spinet piano and bench, which doubled as storage for sheet music, in our seldom-used living room. We, Marilynn and I, were not allowed to go in that designer-decorated room except to practice the piano. My mother was proud to have the piano, and she told everyone who would listen that Abraham Lincoln had one just like ours. I was impressed because I had read and reread the story of Abraham Lincoln's life about 50 times. If he had that same piano, then sprained fingers nearly broken or not, I would practice more. This lasted three more weeks until Mrs. Vans said to my mother that I was a naughty girl with no proclivity for playing the piano and my mother was wasting her money. She was right. Fields came to many of those piano lessons. He saw the injustices. He knew I had talent. He told me many times during our time together that I did not ever have to believe that witch, Mrs. Vans.

He said, "Believe me Sunshine, someday, you will write words to songs and people will sing them. One day we were listening to some wonderful music and Fields asked me to write words to the song and I did. Every time after that, when we would hear music we liked, I would write words to the melody. The music would play and we would break out singing our own original words. I wish I had those words today. I still write words to songs and sing them to Fields. I am grateful to Fields for giving me the music Mrs. Vans tried to steal from my consciousness. Here, remembering Mrs. Vans and the piano lessons, I am in reality remembering that Fields gave me courage, a remarkable faith in myself, and my relationship to music. He also gave me a confidence with words, lest they be in my mind, on the tip of my tongue or interpreting life's complications. Here I am singing to you Fields. I am singing your songs, the ones you gave me assurance would be sung, the ones others are singing to you and to the love shared.

Morning dawned on some of the most spectacular towering mountain peaks I had ever seen. Ferns massed together for miles and miles along the tracks and in open spaces between trees. The colors of green varied, dotted by an occasional glimpse of an illuminated dewdrop. The rays of light made the distant forest look like an ancient kingdom crowned by the sunlight. The train still sounded like Beethoven's Piano Sonata from the night before. The dining car was full, a line of prospective diners protruded from each end, and I was forced to eat a sandwich I had packed at the last minute before leaving to board the train.

As we traveled, the time got closer to seeing Fields, meeting his dad, talking and working out some issues connected with the times we would be together as well as how to deal with the time we had to spend apart.

My mind rambled back to a time when Fields and I were sitting next to each other in the auditorium at our grade school. We always ended up next to each other whether he started at the first of the line with me trailing at the end or not. We gravitated together naturally. An educational film was being shown.

I raised my hand and ever so politely asked the teacher if I could go to the bathroom. The teacher told me that I absolutely would not be excused because I had been given ample time to go to the bathroom earlier and the movie was going to begin in moments. I would not take no for an answer. When a person had to go, a person had to go; no matter how much ample time previously or how soon the movie was beginning. I decided that since the lights were off and Fields was glued to the film, as were the others, I could just pull down my underwear and do my business. It was such a relief.

The film ended and we were all ready to leave the auditorium. Not so fast. The teacher and the principal were surveying something in the front of the auditorium, which I later found out was a puddle of pee. Mine.

The principal asked, "Who peed?" No hands flew into the air in admission. I was certain I would get away with it–how was anyone to know? The lights had been off; there were hundreds of others in the room. How would they be able to guess? Having only nine years of experience, how did I know that the auditorium was designed with an uphill or downhill slant, depending on how you look at it? Actually the way most things are viewed in real life depends on how you look at them. Anyway, the line of wetness delivered the teacher and the principal to my chair, where the line began and ended. I was in very big trouble. I've blocked the rest of the event. I just know I lived to tell it.

I reminded Fields of that time in the auditorium the afternoon of the day before he left to assume his architect position in Seattle. "Do you remember the time I peed in the auditorium and they traced it to me?" I asked.

"Yes, I sure do. I remember that you peed in the sandbox because the teacher said no one was to bother her, positively no one for any reason, or else. I guess you couldn't bother her, so you just did you business right then and there. Gee, Sunshine, you'll probably end up peeing in strange places all over the world." I think I smiled at him, but I have now lived long enough to make his prediction come true.

The train made its stop in Seattle, Washington, and it was time for me to leave. When I first left the train, the station was full of people coming and going; then it began to thin out and I was alone. Fields had not come to meet me and fear took over. I worried that something had happened to him. Something did happen, but not to Fields.

I waited for several hours because I knew that whatever happened, someone would come for me. Two hours and forty minutes later, several trains had come and gone off to other parts of the United States; I was still waiting, tried and true.

While I was waiting, I dragged my valise to a stand serving coffee. The clerk added an extra shot of hot milk, and this turned out to be the most delicious, creamy, badly needed cup of coffee in my memory. It was warm and smooth, sweet and velvety. I am convinced that here at this train station in Seattle, Washington, in the USA, I was one of the first to taste what later was to become a café latte. Years have come and gone, and every time I have had an opportunity to have a café latte, I would sip and be transported back to the day I waited and waited for Fields in the Seattle train station. Each time, the coffee trickles down, each sip equally as good as the first.

Waiting For My Friend

■■■ ■■

"IF SOMEBODY OUTDRAWS YOU, SMILE AND WALK AWAY.
THERE'S PLENTY OF TIME TO LOOK TOUGH WHEN
YOU'RE OUT OF SIGHT."

The truth is, something did happen. Knowing or sensing something happened, not knowing what, and feeling the hunch made me so anxious. I called Fields at the two numbers I had for him. I was about to hail a cab to take me over to his office or his home address. Then I thought if he didn't answer at either place, he wasn't there.

I decided to sit and calm myself because there was nothing I could do but wait. Soon my mind drifted to a time Fields shared with me that his best friend from the team made secret plans. I was away at camp, so I didn't know until a year later about Fields and Tooty. They were going to meet some of the other guys and do what guys do. Fields went out to wait for his friend; he saw him riding by with a fellow friend in a fancy car. He was sure the guy driving the car was one of their buddies. Fields said he tried to hail them, but they just drove on by. Several days passed, and Fields finally had it out with Tooty.

Fields said, "It isn't cool to take off with someone else just because they have a car."

"Yeah, I didn't think you really wanted to go."

"Bull shit, you know I wanted to go; you just wanted to be a big shot and go with the guy with the car."

"No I didn't." said Tooty.

"What am I gonna say here, Tooty. I'll just remember it. I thought we were blood buddies forever."

"We are, pal, we are blood buddies forever."

But they were not. After those early years of boyhood, Tooty went bad, very bad.

I have wondered more than once if he had anything to do with the blow to the left side of Fields' head. I saw flashes of Tooty's face after Fields was gone. I have tried to think back to whether I really saw him somewhere in the wrong place or if he appeared in my mind for no apparent reason. Was it a lost and returned memory? Was Tooty there? Did Fields do something that I didn't know that would make Tooty mad enough to kill? Was Tooty the blood buddy who took Fields' blood forever? I wonder, was the flash of a face I saw in my mind true, was it Tooty or did I invent it to help recover or reclaim Fields' life?

Fields said that Tooty and the car was one incident in his life where his trust was impacted; the incident had taken away some of the glory and the naïveté of youth, of honor, and the admiration and respect he had for friendship. Fields said that his idea of friendship was a positive, non-judgmental thing, and that you should give your friends your true thoughts. He forgave Tooty, but he remembered. He felt friendship was a garden that you entered at your own risk. He said that what Tooty did he would never do to anyone, but in fact he did. Fields was not perfect; he was human. He talked badly about Tooty. He let his feelings be known in all the right places. He was just talking, nothing really bad, so he thought.

I told Fields that the same car incident happened to me. The day I saw my two best girlfriends riding around, smiling and laughing, pleased with each other as they left me in the dust, I complained to my mother. My mother said, "Oh well, honey, maybe they are planning a surprise Sweet Sixteen birthday party for you, and they have to go off and do things for the party."

"How preposterous, Mom."

Four days later, they had a surprise birthday party for me. I felt badly that perhaps I had misjudged them, but I hadn't. They are both exactly the same today as they were then; they do exactly the same things, only I am not the recipient. Fields and I discussed the massive, life-altering loss of trust in friendships we both had. We both felt betrayed, and forever after looked to friendships as betrayals waiting to happen.

Had Fields lived into older age, would he have shed this mistrust, and would he have recovered this slip of self-confidence and this blow to his heart? Would he have realized his own breeches in friendship? Would he have been able to analyze his own personality to see how his values and ideals worked in the world of friendships? Have I lost my mistrust as I have aged?

If Fields were here, I would tell him that I have been able to see myself as a good friend, yet, well able to verbalize my dissatisfaction at some of the actions of others. Fields always wanted me to stand up for myself and not fall victim to the actions of others. He used to call me "The Little Victim." He would be pleased to know that in my sixties, I have come into my own. I do not distrust others because I trust myself. I open my mouth and form questions that put people back in their places so that they are unable to reach me. If I don't want to talk to someone calling on the phone, I don't have to answer, and I don't feel guilty. He would never believe that the name of the person calling you is flashed on the telephone screen and if you don't feel like talking to that person, you can make that decision nearly simultaneously with the flash of the name. There is something so strange about that added state of friendship.

Tooty was single-minded and unwavering in his attempt to make up the wrong Fields felt he had done to him. He left notes, flowers, strings, bows, figurines, pictures, medallions, and his class ring nailed in and tied to the headstone over the grave of our deceased Fields. He never missed Fields' birthday or his own. He took his family on picnics to the gravesite, and they all rallied around, having their celebrations at the headstone of his dead friend.

One of my visits to Fields' grave happened to be during one of Tooty's celebrations. In a whisper mostly to myself, I said, "Fields, I hope you know that Tooty could not have done more to honor your friendship. He is here every birthday and every holiday hoping you can see that he is determined to restore the trust he broke so long ago."

I will always remember as soon as I finished my sentences I saw a flash on the north side of the park. I walked in that direction, wandering purposely towards the north wall. The flash was there again and I began to follow it. I knew this image to truly be Fields in the same way I had always known him. He was a brightly lit image; behind him was the dark shadowed part of the park. He looked sheepishly into my eyes as he had always done when he wanted an answer to a question. Had he asked a question, had he seen Tooty's celebration? What did Fields want of me? What did he always want of me? He took my hands and placed them on him in a dance position, placing his hands to fit. We began to dance. This is the dance I will remember because of the twinkles and mist enveloping us. We moved together and apart. We started ever so slowly, together leaning, warming, and gliding towards a spot where we went around in circles dizzying ourselves. Fields was smiling. I was happy knowing that I was with Fields again. The dance built to a strong crescendo and then, slowed down to a gentle moving closer and closer together. He put his finger to his lips and then placed his finger and the kiss on my mouth. I heard him whisper, "Stay away from Tooty." Then, Fields backed away from me and from the scene in the cemetery. He was gone, but he was to return several more times to repeat our dance in the cemetery park filling me with the power of love given and returned. After our first dance, I began to again wonder and at some point wholeheartedly believe why Tooty was so attentive and so repentant at the site of Fields' grave.

Still, sometimes I see a flitting image of Tooty peering at the death scene from behind buildings on the street where Fields lost his life. Why do these images come and go, flit in and out plaguing my mind and causing discordance and query?

Jarring me to my present senses and bringing me back to the train station was a howling "yoo hoo." I was surprised to see Eugenia coming to meet me; I dropped the empty coffee cup and stood up to meet her embrace.

"How are you Eugenia? Did something happen to Fields?"

"Fields is fine, but Martin Fields has had a stroke and is in a deep coma."

For an instant, I had forgotten that Martin Fields could be Fields and Eugenia's dad as well as a long-lost husband. I felt concerned. I was confused as to what to do next and how to help in this situation.

Eugenia steered me towards a waiting taxi. I didn't ask any questions, and we drove in silence until we stopped in front of the hospital. We still didn't speak. We just moved across the seat, opened the doors, slipped out into the entrance of the hospital, opened the large double doors and walked down the dingy, cramped hallway full of people coughing, hacking out germs and bantering back and forth with the nurses as they passed by. We turned right, then left. We entered a small rickety elevator and rose to the 4th floor. We exited and turned to the left. The halls were brighter looking, but the place had a feeling of various stages of dying; hidden in some deeper recesses, there must surely be hope and recovery.

We entered a small waiting room with several leather couches and a wing chair. People occupied all of the seats and several leaned against the walls.

I saw Fields. He came over and said nothing, but leaned against my arm. His heart was beating wildly through his shirt, through his arm muscle, into my shirt and into my arm. I could feel Fields just the way I had always felt him. I knew just what he would say if the words had come, but Fields and I needed no words. I could feel the weight of his questions and his thoughts burning through his skin into mine.

These are the questions he transferred through his skin to mine: Is the man in Room 2131 my dad? Is he the man I came to meet, perhaps never to know as blood of my blood? Will this man pass into eternal life taking his secrets with him? What should we say to these people who are here, these people who are his family, too? How will I ever know the truth about Martin Fields? Will I ever know if he is bound to me? Are his children my brother and sister? Are they my people? To these and more questions Fields needed answers. I felt I had a key to open avenues for Fields if I dare to break that promise I had made to myself.

I wanted to ask Eugenia if she knew anything about a carved box in her childhood home, but if I asked, I would have to use the key. And what would it open? I asked nothing.

Days and weeks passed. Nothing was established. From day to day the man lying in hospital bed 2131 never changed. His expressions stayed the same, his facial hair either did not grow or the nurses are expert barbers in addition to their nursing duties. His weight stayed the same, his eyes, closed to the world, letting in light but masking his brain. He was a man, just a man lying there.

Fields would leave the room after a visitation and climb the stairs to the outside rooftop access. He told me later that he would sit Indian fashion for the next few hours recollecting images of past days when his fractured family was whole. He said he was able to slip into the past and bring back images of a day when he was a little boy; he could only hope that they were images of this Martin Fields as his dad.

Fields said there was a dad in those images, and he was driving everyone to the county fair. Fields said the imagery in his mind blurred and melted. Each character dissolved and liquefied and interchanged; the only clear image was that of a clown loudly dressed and thickly made up. The frozen smile and the big red nose scared Fields out of his wits. In Fields' fantasy, he soiled his pants. Still in muted scenes, Mr. Dad lost his temper and slammed his fists into a pole. He dragged the kids, Mrs. Mom following close by as a mother hen does, all the while trying to sooth Mr. Dad's ruffled feathers. Dad dragged and slammed the kids into the car and pushed Mom into the passenger seat.

Fields told me that he remembered Dad's big hands turning the wheel of the car in the direction of home. He remembered the tears he shed, the smell from his pants and the words, "All your fault!"

One day we entered Martin Fields' hospital room

just as a team of doctors arrived. They told Fields that this man in a coma, had blood type O. Fields' blood type was O, but brother Brock and sister Eugenia had blood type B. I knew Fields' mother had blood type B. If DNA testing had already been invented, we could have been assured one way or the other, but the blood type was the only clue.

Martin's other family was waiting as well. The tension in the room was like thick fog. I saw them all through a hazy film. It was clear that the other family members did not want Fields to be there. They were afraid to exchange too many empty words; they seemed to see Fields as an opponent. If the man in the coma were Fields' father, would this news change the cause and actions of the others? Would it change Fields' power and actions towards the man in the coma and his family?

Why was this game of silence being played? Would anyone stand to win a prize if they embraced? Was knowledge of one's father a win or lose counteraction or a power struggle? If it were true, would Fields then belong to this new family? Would they become a part of him? The unspoken words and the glances through the film and the fog told their own stories about the people in that hospital room. Finally, Fields broke the tension and went over to hug Mrs. Fields.

"I hope we all come out of this okay," he said.

"You are a nice boy," she said.

"Thank you," he said.

Mr. Martin Fields

■■■ ■■

"WHEN YOU LOSE THE GAME, DON'T LOSE THE LESSON."

While talking to this family, Fields discovered that the man in Room 2131 was a very independent man full of contradictions, issues and an incapacity to show his love in a demonstrative way. His wife said he would hold back for fear of becoming too emotional and blowing his aloof laid-back demeanor. The Martin Fields that Fields had known in the household of his childhood was a figure to reckon with at all times. Fields had a watchful eye and observed everything; he remembered that he could tell what his father was thinking by the look on his face. Even if he hadn't known what his father was thinking, he thought he had. He knew that sometimes he thought his father was thinking one thing and by the man's actions he knew he was wrong. Dead wrong.

His father had seldom yelled or raised his voice, but Fields remembered that when his father's words ran together, when he made statements that didn't have anything to do with what was actually going on, when he started drumming his fingers on the furniture, he, Fields, was out the door as fast as thoughts could cross synapses and spread along dendrites.

Fields told me that he could close his eyes and remember his Martin Fields at home. One night his father was smoking and drinking. That combination made him perceive many a thing that was not true. On this particular night, when Fields was nine and his brother was sixteen, Dad came after them in an angry fit. He grabbed at Fields and beat his face and neck. While he was knocking Fields down, his brother made a getaway. Mr. Fields' breath came in heavy gasps full of spit, making the image unforgettable.

He yelled, "Fletcher, you god-damned thief, you

stole my watch."

"What watch?"

"That there watch on the table. You took it, you little 'cuss."

"Dad, I never saw a watch. You don't have a watch. You don't need a watch. You always know what time it is, no matter when we ask you." Fields said his dad came at him swinging both fists, and when his right fist slammed into the wall, it made a hole right through to the room on the other side. While his dad was trying to get his hand loose, Fields scrambled to his feet and bolted out the front door. He started running and didn't stop until he hit the sea wall that fronted the bay. Fields told me he slept out in some bushes that night and had never ever been so cold or afraid.

"From that day on, I was never cold or afraid again. I learned that fear was only being afraid."

He told me he conquered being afraid that night by using calming words to talk himself down from panic into a normal state. He taught himself some words that triggered a relaxed state and fell asleep. He told me some of the words he used from then on were circle, relax, automatic, wonderful, message, mellow, and Sunshine. He said he tried to picture a message from me that made him laugh. Fields learned the art of reaching his subconscious mind by picturing a message from me making him laugh. I still remember that with joy.

I know that from then on Fields never spent any time in his home when he knew that his father was about. When his dad would come in the front door, Fields would go out the back. When his old man was asleep, Fields would creep back, go to his room, and sleep with one eye on the door and his nicked and dented baseball bat beside him under the covers. Fields never considered the bat a deadly weapon, just one that would protect him and allow a getaway. He told me he knew when his dad got up and he knew when his dad was washing, shaving, pissing, pooping, eating breakfast; when he was out of the door, Fields would rise and do the same.

Now Fields was faced with a man lying comatose, his father or not his father? He looked deeply into the closed tearing eyes, saw the facial hair sticking straight out, and said he wanted to poke the sagging jowls. If the man could open his eyes, Fields would see those tiger marbled eyes, the thing he remembers most strongly. They would serve as portholes into his passing.

I knew Fields possessed a hidden weapon, his shielded emotions. He would not let himself feel. If this man were not his father, Fields would turn and walk out of the hospital free of hostility, vengeance and hatred. He would not search again, but let the knowing and the not knowing continue to shape his character and deepen the creases of his being.

"Why am I here looking for this long-lost father?" Fields asked me late one afternoon.

"Because you think you will solve some unresolved issues, but you will not."

"How do you know so much?"

"Look Fields," I said, "You were sort of railroaded into meeting this man, then when he fell into a coma, things got bigger and bigger, and your need to talk with him was inflated so you stayed. I've certainly had my issues with this whole thing, remember?"

Fields tilted his head and sighed. The next few moments we spent in silence and remembrance.

"Yeah, I thought if I got to know his other family it

would help me, but they don't want me here, Sunshine."

"I know and they don't pull any punches about it. Hey, why don't you start asking them questions and find out if this guy was like your dad?"

"You got something there."

"Okay, tomorrow start talking and asking. I wonder if they will be honest, or have they begun to immortalize and martyr him already?"

"Do you think we can tell what is truth and what might be martyrdom?" asked Fields.

I remained mute. I wanted to tell him that we could tell, but I really didn't know. Telling martyrdom from reality is something for the experts, and even they don't always know.

The next afternoon in Martin Fields' hospital room, the ice broke.

"Here you are," said Mrs. Fields.

"We are glad you're here," said Jared.

"I'm glad I am here," said Fields.

"Let me ask you," said Mrs. Fields, "how did you come to know about Martin?"

Fields explained that a man he worked with thought

he was the spitting image of this Martin Fields, who belonged to his club. Fields said he thought he would like to know if in fact this man was his father.

Jared asked, "If my dad is your dad, what do you plan to do about it?"

"I haven't thought about that, Jared. I just thought about finding out."

"Do you want any money?" asked Mrs. Fields.

Fields reeled back and opened his mouth. He hesitated, trying to get his thoughts into words. The whole room was still as if everyone was holding their breath. "I don't need any money. I have money and I make money."

"Oh."

"One more thing, I kinda' got caught up in this finding my dad thing. Maybe I found another family. I wouldn't mind that, you know. I really wouldn't mind that at all."

Mrs. Fields' eyes softened and the lines on her brow disappeared. She leaned against the bed and shot a full smile at Fields. "I wouldn't mind either." I was so proud of the dignified way Fields put their minds at ease.

Jared excused himself, kissed his mother, patted his sister's shoulder, smoothed his dad's forehead, shook Fields' hand, winked at me and left us. We began to ask the two remaining family members about the man so peacefully comatose. Yes, they had begun to immortalize and martyr him, but for now it seemed natural and necessary.

As we left the hospital, the street was packed with people milling and jabbering about something, in the middle of the road. We had a destination–hunger dictated. The crowd moved with us, pushing and pulling at the same time. At the corner, there was an accident. We didn't want to see it and tried our best to skirt it but found ourselves instead with a front-row view. We saw four or five vehicles with bumper scrapes, all the drivers and their passengers standing beside their cars.

"Look," I said tugging Fields' sleeve, "there's Jared." We rushed up to him. I said,

"This is so incredible to see you here, we just saw you and..."

"We had some trouble right away after I got picked up. I mean we crashed a little."

He had a tiny split on his forehead and a swollen lip. He had been a passenger in the seat next to his friend who looked fine except for being distraught and anxious. We gave considerable effort to see if there was anything we could do to immediately help the situation. The particulars would have to be sorted out later by insurance companies, lawyers and the participants themselves.

"Would you like to join us for lunch?" Fields asked the two young men.

"I need to take my car somewhere and get it checked out," said Jared's friend.

Jared checked with his friend and they talked back and forth, nodding to each other and Jared turned to us and said," I'll join you," said Jared, so we took him with us to find something to appease the hunger gods.

Fields and Jared fell into a steady conversation back and forth that continued once we were seated in a small shop that served sandwiches. My thoughts wandered in and out; I had a funny conversation with myself. I had never thought of my needs as gods and goddesses guiding me. Early civilizations did and they seemed to get it right. They worshipped the sun, of course, because the sun is responsible for all of life. What about the moon god? The ancient Incas believed that gold was sweat from the sun and silver were tears from the moon. What about diamonds? Maybe they hadn't ever seen one. How could I have a god for something I didn't know existed? Perhaps that is why I perceive God, as an all-knowing entity taking care of and guiding me in all that I do not know, cannot see, hear, or feel.

Then I switched into thinking about Greek and Roman mythological gods. They covered the territory. They had gods and goddesses for thunder, rain, war, youth, love, beauty, rainbows, fertility, sun, moon, stars, cattle, seeds, childbirth, wind, victory, pleasure, fortune and health. They had gods and goddesses for emotions and behavior. They left nothing to chance. Neither shall I, I vowed to myself.

The shop we had chosen for food served the most succulent brisket sandwiches on the face of this planet, or so said the sign.

"I have never eaten in a downtown restaurant before," considered Jared

"I have and lived to tell it."

"Do you think this is a problem?"

"Nope."

We placed our order for three of their sensational brisket sandwiches with a fellow named Johnny. He was a jovial man with a wide, mustached smile revealing perfectly set teeth. Fields asked Johnny why this was the most famous place in town. Johnny loved to talk. He said that his father had the shop before him, and he was planning to give it to his son someday, but Uncle Arthur had come to call earlier than he expected. It turned out that what he meant by Uncle Arthur was the onset of arthritis. He said it was very bad in his family; his thumbs already didn't work like they used to, and his knees were getting bad.

Johnny said that he worried that the secrets in the cooking of the brisket would be lost. He said that he figured a way to get the word out and people were coming.

"You think you want to share your secret?" asked Fields

Johnny was willing and ready to give away his juicy brisket secrets knowing that, hard as you tried, you couldn't equal the mood, atmosphere, and, most importantly, the taste and consistency that marked his success. His willingness to share his knowledge of the brisket only enhanced customers' desire to experience his hospitality.

"You get the biggest, puffiest brisket you can find," Johnny explained. "You rub it with crushed garlic and a very special ingredient, Season All salt. Nothing fancy, just the brand Season All. Then you crank the oven up to 450 degrees for about an hour or until you have not quite burned the outer layer of the brisket. Then you turn the oven down to 325 degrees and let it cook for four, five or six hours.

"You'll know when it's done," he continued. "Just look at it and the brisket almost talks to you. If you have to, you can poke it. Let it have a rest for about thirty minutes and you're ready to slice and serve."

"Thanks, Johnny."

I said, "I'm sure going to try it."

"My pleasure folks. I'll be bringing your food out in a few minutes."

While we waited for our lunch, Fields and I tried getting Jared to talk about his family. Jared was seventeen years old, quite good looking, thin, and had pimples that needed to be controlled; his hands were small, his feet big and his head flat. I hadn't noticed any of this before we were sitting in such close quarters because he had a perpetual smile on his face. All you really saw of Jared was his smile. It was not one of those open smiles where you get a powerhouse of teeth back at you, an open grin. His eyes twinkled, making for an overall appealing look.

Jared was always quiet. In fact, until today, I never heard him speak. His mother Envita and sister Suzanne always did most of the talking. They were always guarded when anyone outside of the family was present, as if they have something to hide. Very little information about the Fields family ever came from the spoken word.

What we observed was that Envita never touched her children and would continually move her self out of their reach. The children never touched their father or each other. Jared had made himself approachable with his grin, his youth and his desire to have Fields as a brother.

During lunch, Fields and I talked and Jared listened. The topic we chose seemed an unlikely one to share with someone who didn't know us well, but it just popped out of our mouths in puffs, maybe because we needed to recount it to each other. We were getting to know Jared and creating a brotherhood, but those facts slipped out of our consciousness and we just slipped into ourselves. Jared on the other hand, got to hear and feel us in a way few others have seen. The conversation began to take shape.

"Remember the time we got saved?" I asked Fields.

"Oh, I will never forget it."

"What were we thinking?"

"I was thinking that if I got saved, then I would be safe."

"They didn't say that."

"No, but they said I would go to heaven, and I still believe them on that one."

One day Fields and I had run away from school because my teacher Mrs. Jefferson was very mean to me and dug her nails into my flesh so hard that my arm started bleeding. I poked my head into Fields' room and beckoned him out. He made the necessary bathroom arrangements with his teacher and we were on our way. I talked him into going to the corner market for an ice cream and then, maybe, to his house.

Along the way a divine intervention popped up. I tripped and fell, scraping my knee. There was lots of blood, and when I saw the wound I started to bawl my eyes out. Fields tried to pick me up, but no luck. It so happened that we were in front of a small, well kept, inviting church. The doors were open for business, and while Fields was trying to console me, out came some pretty important-looking grown-ups. They helped Fields carry me into the main chapel where we all sat towards the front. The doctoring of body and soul began.

The lady, in a blue suit with a flower on her shoulder and a sweet smell, went to the kitchen and brought back some water, cloths and a lovely big bandage. You know how kids love bandages, and this was a big one. I was thinking maybe this was paradise and angels were surrounding me because I was already dead. Then the drill began and it was quite simple.

"Do you kids want to go to heaven?"

We both nodded in agreement.

"Well, then, we can arrange that right now. If you accept Jesus Christ as your personal savior, then you will go to heaven. Can you do this?"

I would have done anything to be able to go to heaven, and that was the truth. But I had no idea what the man who was talking meant for sure. Later, Fields told me he had already been saved, so he was already going to heaven; on the other hand, to make sure he really got to heaven, he figured he should be saved again.

The man, who had huge blue eyes, bluer than any ocean, said a few loud words praising the Lord, and then he said, "In the name of the Father, the Son and the Holy Ghost." Water splashed from somewhere; at the time, I thought maybe the roof had a leak, too young to realize that it wasn't even raining.

Before sending us on our way, the man patted each of us on the tops of our heads and asked the pretty, sweet-smelling lady walk us back to school. To this day, when-ever I'm in doubt, I can feel those droplets of rain on my forehead, and I know I am safe and I am saved.

I walked back into Mrs. Jefferson's room knowing something special. I knew I was going to heaven; she could poke me and shove me, even kill me, and I was going to heaven. That single moment in my life freed me to be strong because I would always be moving toward heaven and perhaps another life.

I don't know if I still believe in heaven and hell. I

keep a faith because I know I am, and we all are, going somewhere. Fields said that he thought we were saved together because someday we will be together. Being Jewish and knowing what I know, I believe that being saved converted my shackles, which were locked by fear of the unknown. At that instant of melding, my life became filled with bounteous opportunities, releasing the limitations I had collected along the way, and unchaining my heart.

I have never been sorry I was saved. I think about that day so many times and feel grateful. I smile when I recognize it for what it was. I smile because no one else knows the secret that illuminates my way. I would never give up the culture and beliefs that are my birthright, but I feel that adding to them is glory in its own right.

I thanked Jared for listening. I thanked God for the memory.

Jared's Revelation

■■■■■

"LETTING THE CAT OUT OF THE BAG IS A WHOLE LOT EASIER THAN PUTTING IT BACK IN."

Jared was willing and actually seemed to relish the idea of sharing with Fields. He loved Fields as a brother nearly the instant they met. Both of them wanted this to be true kinship, but for now it would be love, brotherhood and sharing.

"I am not Martin Fields' son. Suzanne is not his daughter. We are son and daughter of Envita and Horatio Hadrian. They married when my mother was only fifteen and my father was thirty-six. They crossed over the border from Mexico before we were born. I was born in

San Clemente, Suzanne in Salinas. They moved to San Jose for a number of years. My father was gone by the time Suzanne was three. He didn't die. He just wandered off one night, said he'd be back, and never showed up again. My mother moved to Watsonville, where she met Martin Fields."

Fields wanted to know everything, but he drew in a long breath, closed his eyes and rested a moment as he collected his thoughts and formulated his questions.

"When did you know about your real dad?"

"In the hospital."

"You didn't know anything about Dad Hadrian until the hospital?

"Right."

"Why did she tell you now, I wonder. Why did she wait?"

"You don't need to wonder; she's weak now and scared. She wants us to have someone if Dad goes. She wants us to search for our real dad. She needs someone, too."

Jared toyed with the leftover crumbs from his sandwich and ran his fingers over the condensation on his empty glass. Quiet moments passed.

"I know you noticed some tension between all of us. I hope this explains some of the stuff going on."

Fields was ready to talk. "Hey, maybe this guy is my dad and maybe not, but I sure as hell don't know. Tell me, what was he like as a dad."

"Good dad. "

"Good means what, huh?   Did he listen to you, did he help you with homework, build model airplanes with you--I dunno, man--what did he do?   Tell me something, man."

Jared's breath came in short spurts and finally, after some time elapsed, he answered, "Dad came home late lots of nights, but he had to work late. He is the owner of Hardwick's Swap Shop a hardware store on Roosevelt Way NE in Seattle. He goes in later in the afternoon but has to stay until closing most nights. I could walk there and I did lots of nights. It's cool to see him working. He is so busy; he only has time for a half smile and a wink. He took us out to dinner a couple of times, you know, the whole family, but it always got screwed up. He would end up in a talking marathon that lasted for days. He's a nice guy, but it kind of feels good that he is not my dad because now I have a chance not to keep the angry stuff in my head."

"Angry stuff?"

"Yeah, he's an angry guy, mainly."

"Did he hit you guys?" asked Fields tentatively.

"Yeah, sure."

I remember the brilliant and unmistakably unique color of Fields' dad's eyes. They were the tiger marbled eyes just like mine. I wondered if Jared would be able to tell us the color of his dad's eyes. This could solve this mystery more rapidly than any other method. Why hadn't I thought of the solution weeks before, when the journey began? No time for should-have could-have thoughts.

"Jared, what color are your dad's eyes?" I asked.

"Blue, blue like the mountain sky on a sunny day."

"Sure?"

"Sure."

I was stunned at the new information. Fields kept talking with Jared and didn't make the connection. I couldn't wait to tell him. Lunch was over, and I stood up. We hugged Jared and he hugged back, smiling. He said he was going to find his friend and find out more about the car and the accident.

"See you guys," he said and took off down the street.

"See you, Jared."

I was so full of my discovery that I couldn't wait another second. "Let's go back to the hospital?" I said.

"Why?"

"Need to find out something?"

"Did you forget something there?"

"Maybe."

"Okay let's go, but I've got to get back to work. I got things to do, babe."

"Nothing more important than this."

"You sound gritty."

"Determined. Look, do you remember your dad had the marbled eyes of a tiger? Do you remember you told me many times my eyes were the color of your dad's eyes?"

"I remember, now that you reminded me. Yes, I do remember."

"Jared is way too poetic about the blue eyes, as blue as the mountain skies on a sunny day. Right? We don't have time to worry why he is so poetic about the eyes, but if it is true, blue, I mean, if this Martin Fields has blue eyes, then you can walk away free. He won't be your dad if he has eyes, blue as the mountain skies."

"Yeah, walk away free. I really do not want to be free, maybe I do, maybe part of me wants to be a part of him, part of them"

We walked back to the hospital quickly, both of us thinking blue or marbled tiger-eyes. Fields said, "Sunshine, I feel so close to something. It's warm; there is something moving me along, like a big hand in the middle of my back."

"Me too."

We walked stride for stride. Our minds were on the same plane. I was remembering that Fields said he would go out a knowing man no matter whether this man was or wasn't his dad. He just needed to know for sure; then he could leave behind the resentment and the bitterness of his previous family life and get on to a new dawning. I believed him. I even thought there would be a chance for us. We loved each other and perhaps we would create a life together.

We rounded the corner and headed towards the hospital entrance. We opened the doors and took the elevator up to the 4th floor. I had a head start and waited for nothing. I walked past an attending nurse, pulled up one of Martin Fields' eyelids and peered into a bright blue eye, blue as sunny skies on mountaintops, just as Jared had said. Fields, bent close next to me, gulped air and stammered, "Blue."

"Let's go, Fields. You are now going to show up for the first day of the rest of your life."

Fields didn't wait for the elevator; he bounded down the steps, and when I heard the last of his steps, I knew he was gone into a world I could not be part of, and one I could not participate in.

I didn't see Fields for the rest of the day and night. He was sorting out what he needed to know about himself and how to begin again. What was unique about Fields' new self-knowledge was that he couldn't use guidebooks to recreate himself, to figure out how to deal with alarm bells going off with each new encounter or how to bend like bamboo.

Bamboo is such a realistic plant. It is designed so

that when the wind blows it can bend to manage the force. Bamboo has been known to be the only thing left standing after a hurricane has devastated large swatches of land. Fields had learned to bend like bamboo years and years ago; he just needed some time to rid himself of the toxic factors barring his way to remember bending. Life is full of wind, and one must learn to bend, to create durability, flexibility and strength. Where bamboo grows, it grows in abundance. Bamboo can live and grow in any season; therefore, not only bending when the time is right but adapting, as well, are qualities humans should strive to share with bamboo.

Fields knew that bamboo spreads and has runners that divide, creating new growth that can easily take any planting space, no matter the size. We broke off a piece of bamboo from a neighbor's pot of giant pandas and planted it in a tiny space behind Fields' house. It didn't take long for us to see firsthand the properties and assets of bamboo. We cut pieces and gave them to our friends. I'll bet our old Downey Street neighborhood is overrun with bamboo plants and runners.

We knew Martin Fields of Seattle survived, and we

knew that he did not belong to Fields and Fields did not belong to him. Fields had little blame or little regret. Before he had time to quantify or qualify his feelings about the Martin Fields dilemma, his mother caused another major disruption in his life.

His Auntie Ruth called Fields home. His mother was sinking further into a consumptive type of disease. She had been staring into space for years, unable to remember the past, let alone deal functionally in the present. Auntie Ruth, her sister, had been taking care of her daily needs. Fields told his firm that he would be back soon and would keep in touch. I accompanied him back to Downey Street. This time Fields was going in search of his mother.

Auntie Ruth was used to guarding her words and it was hard for Fields to pry loose from her lips the details of the past year of his mother's life. What he did learn, did not surprise him. The Mom had fallen into a daily routine but soon was unable to carry on. Auntie Ruth had come to live and care for her sister as if she were her baby. The Mom had turned into a baby. She whined, cried, cooed, drooled, and soiled her diapers. She had nothing to share with Fields except a glance in his direction and a baby-like, open-mouthed smile.

Fields was determined to stay for a while to see what he could do to help the situation. He saw that Auntie Ruth worked very hard and was on call twenty-four hours a day. He wanted to give her some free time. As it turned out, Auntie Ruth had no one and nothing else, nor anywhere to spend her free time, so Fields was the one with free time to spend.

Lessons Revisited

"LIVE A GOOD, HONORABLE LIFE. THEN WHEN YOU GET OLDER AND THINK BACK, YOU'LL ENJOY IT A SECOND TIME."

When we returned to San Francisco, Fields stayed with his mother, and I stayed with mine. Fields still had no idea where his father might be or even if he was alive, whereas, my father still lived with my mother in the house on Downey Street. My father was strong, shrewd in business, handsome, squared off and bespectacled. I inherited all of his physical and mental characteristics. He didn't know it because I was female, and girls in our family were to be looked at, patted on the head and adored in a baby sort of way. They were not allowed intellectual discussions and weren't asked their opinions on anything other than the weather.

I was twelve at the time when I became interested in the stock market. I saw an opportunity to buy Bonanza Airlines and had a sixth sense that it was going to go up. My father consented to buy it for me. Sure enough, within a few months the stock skyrocketed, and we sold it at a tidy little profit.

I was on Cloud Nine and scoured the stock section of the newspaper for weeks after my windfall. When I found another stock I wanted to buy, my father put the brakes on and said that girls had other things to do and to think about. My stock and bond days were over; my new career plummeted.

Fields asked his mother many times about his father and where he may be living, but his mother was unable to enlighten him or even give him any clues. He decided to be content with the way things had turned out and gave up all desire to find any more evidence that would send him on a chase to a possible truth. He let it lie.

When events were demanding and full of stress, Fields and I both employed the screen door effect we learned years ago on Haight, before it was "The Haight," from a tall bearded guy with a bald crown and hair coming down in cascades from the ring around the bald bowl that graced the top of his head. His name was Mandeep, which he assured everyone had a special meaning, which was, "Lamp of the mind." He taught us that the meaning of his name signified not only strength of mind, but also that by having custody of a lighted lamp; we would be showered with prestige and distinction.

According to Mandeep, all of us give kindness to those in need at times, and whenever we see the icon signifying a lighted lamp, we are able to see into the moment and receive our just rewards. If you see a lighted lamp in your dreams, you are going to experience luck with a relationship of a personal nature; luck with economics, career and travel, and general good health. Lamps in history are legendary. "One if by land, two if by sea."

Mandeep's major goal was to inform everyone about the screen door effect. He would hammer it home following each lecture. I can still hear him now. "The screen door effect is most effective and can be the key to living your life without collecting the force of your own problems or the problems of everyone around the globe. When full-force winds blow against a solid door, that door will try to resist the force. When you remove the solid door and replace it with a screen door, the winds blow through, causing relatively little damage due to force. Try it.

"Picture your own self as a solid force sloughing off unwanted stimuli. Oh, how it hurts and causes stresses and strains on the *solid* you. Your body collects the aches and pains of living solidly. When you mentally exchange the solid door for a screen door, the forces blow through you, causing little pain and leaving no evidence of inhabitation. You don't have to collect and store pain. Use the screen door effect."

Fields and I went to Mandeep's sessions often, and then one day he wasn't there. He never returned. Mandeep was the first of many gurus who frequently stopped in The Haight over the years.

In the days of my youth, I made and sold bead necklaces. I would get a little extra money and I would spend it on beads. The beads began to take on meanings of their own. Each bead was unique and different. I met a woman from Oregon who made little individual clay beads; no two were ever the same, yet they blended nicely when formed into a necklace. As my hands worked, the beads formed their own distinctive, one-of-a-kind masterpiece, as I was unconsciously transported into other realms of exploration.

Picture yourself in your chair at home, and the next moment you're soaring like a helium balloon in mid-air. You are totally in the moment, fully focused and concentrating in that instant. You move slightly and the instant is gone. Not that you want to stay in any of the moments your transportation carries you through, but the carrying and the transporting is the time your mind needs to heal wounds and shave off scars. These are the lessons I learned in the beads.

I learned how to live in the moment, no matter how overwhelming, disheartening or astonishingly brilliant it might be, it is always the moment and always your reality. Many of us share the ability to space out and look into the future. Some of us were taught to meditate. We were told to take time out to think, ponder and mull things over in our minds to promote better health, get a better job, be happier later on; always, we were taught to look further a field. The future is easy thinking because it isn't real. If you are always not real, always in the future, then you feel on shaky ground. You are not sure of things as they are.

I am not suggesting you drop the future; I'm asking you to replace it with what is happening right now, right in the moment. It's much harder to be in the moment, looking at the space and time you occupy. Practice it. Begin to notice whether you are here right now or off thinking of how it should be, could be. Continue to meditate, but do it in the present tense. Thinking in the present tense will bring a whole new you into the future.

Many months after I sold some of my first necklaces, a lady came to me wearing one of my necklaces filled with antiques, bones, and hand-designed and fired beads. The necklace looked exceptionally impressive on her, or was it my pride in seeing someone wearing my necklace?

"I love the idea that this here necklace is magic," she told me.

"Tell me how?" I asked.

"Ever since I bought this necklace I had good luck. Hey, I'm pregnant and we've been trying for years. That's not just magic—it's a miracle."

"How wonderful. I am so pleased. Thank you for telling me such good news."

"That's not all. I got money now, I didn't have much before I met you and bought one of your necklaces."

"Really?"

"Yeah, I want to buy all the stuff you have. I'm gonna leave you one 'cause I want you to have luck and magic, too."

"Okay, you can have your pick."

She looked at all of the necklaces I had hanging on a wire, taking her time. "Okay, this one is yours. Please, please wear it."

I have worn it ever since and wouldn't trade this beaded magical necklace for any newly minted diamond strand.

Fields spent the next three weeks at home with his mother. She was in and out of this world. I visited often. Every time I went into the kitchen in the Fields' home, I had to pause and look at the gold-framed saying torn from a book a long time ago, still hanging over the window that looked out onto the yard. It's a quote from Robert Frost: "Two roads diverged in a wood, and, I took the one less traveled by. And that has made all the difference."

I don't think it has made a difference for Fields or anyone else in his family, because no one has ever mentioned reading it. But it has made a significant difference to me. I read that plaque during all of my growing-up years and I have done as it says. Those roads have challenged and changed my life. I've already told you about some of them.

Fields' mother fell into a pattern of screaming all day. She didn't know she was screaming according to the doctor; it was just the progression in the deterioration of her mind. Fields' Aunt Bessie came to help with The Mom for a while to help him and Auntie Ruth care for her. He knew that this was the beginning of a long ending, but he needed to get away for a while to gain some peace. He expressed to both of his aunts his appreciation for helping so much and confessed his need to get away. They agreed to help each other take care of things at home while he was gone.

Fields' Notes

"THE BIGGEST TROUBLEMAKER YOU'LL PROBABLY EVER HAVE TO DEAL WITH WATCHES YOU SHAVE HIS FACE IN THE MIRROR EVERY MORNING."

Fields' notebook lay on the coffee table for months. His mother had given it to me the day after he passed. She came to our door with a glimmer of recognition in her dulled eyes. She had been through some illogical, unreasonable times, but this must have been the worst for her. Even though Fields' mother had foggy, moments in a maze she still had times when she was lucid and strongly aware of her actions, and the life around her.

She said, "Fields wanted you to have his book. You

can see him on every page. When you see him, don't forget to tell me."

Fields had written on the front cover:

Down on my knees

Devout

Knowing never to have been born

Does never have to die

Living wholly is

Asking the Divine for intervention.

Left in some obscure corner

To be found

By divinity and serenity,

He knows, never profane

He knows to refrain,

His calling is for her ears only.

Be ever present, petitioning.

I looked at that book on the table day after day, and
was afraid to open it. Six months after his death, the day
dawned like very few others. The wind blew fiercely, shaking windows and rattling everything in its path. A good
thing about wind is that it clears the air and simultane-

ously clears some of the webs you have been collecting between your ears. My grandmother used to tell us that the wind didn't blow that often in some parts of the world because people kept the cobwebs cleaned up and that it blew hard and often in other parts because people let the cobwebs build up, especially the ones between their ears. She said that after a good blowing, people did their best thinking.

I promised myself the first time I walked past Fields' book that morning that I would give it my attention before that windy day ended. It was dusk, the sunset producing pink clouds searching for their places, when I remembered my promise.

I picked up Fields' book and opened it to the first page. He wrote, "Did you ever notice that conversations with a crazy person are so very interesting until you realize that they never do quite get to the point."

Fields always wore a bracelet made by a friend of his. It was handcrafted from a sterling silver spoon pilfered from his mother's set of serving silver. He mentioned the bracelet in his notebook. He said," The bracelet is a symbol of bondage and slavery. It is connected somehow to self-worth. It is rounded and feeds back into itself. It is a connection to you, sort of like your own portable umbilical cord. You create and receive power of the present through the belief in the bracelet. There are charm bracelets that dangle your life's history and get caught on loops and threads that hang from your clothing. They get tangled in other people's clothing, so you have to steer clear of getting too tangled up. There are friendship bracelets, bead, mineral, crystal, bead, silver, gold and diamond ones, too. You can make a bracelet out of most anything. My neighbor girl made a bracelet by braiding together leaves from the park together. Sunshine's bracelets have a healing quality to them. People want to wear her bead necklaces and bracelets."

Field's book also included drawings. One is an architectural rendering of a modern building with a sign that reads, Lucky Healing Bead Business. He even designed a leaflet that read, "Be the first to get an original healing bracelet that feeds back into itself and, therefore, you get all the benefits. Manufacturer's guarantee comes with every item purchased."

His notebook goes on to say, "Each item is made to

order and no two are alike. Be surprised to see what our bead maniacs put in your personal item. Send us twenty-five cents for postage, along with four dollars and ninety-five cents for a guaranteed-to-change-your-life bracelet or necklace."

I laughed out loud when I read, "Be sure to include your name, address, telephone number, height, weight, sex, hair color, eye color, and mother's maiden name. If you wish to give some personal information about the recipient, it would be helpful in determining your order." It was signed; The Bead Factory, and it gave an address I didn't recognize. I spent the next hour in tears.

Fields wrote about Cousin Sisyphus. As I read more, I came to realize that he was in fact citing The Myth of Sisyphus. He wrote, "It is said that Cousin Sisyphus has done something to anger the gods. It is not a bad thing, but he is in the throes of enjoying his life, with the sun on his back, the clear lake at his side, the sparkling waters dancing and casting back his own joys, when he is summoned. He smiles and laughs out loud. He is in love with the world and its pleasures. He knows there is torment and pain waiting for him, if not death. He sees the depths of the underworld coming up to meet him.

He dreams of a rock with the weight of suffering, pain and distress in every fragment. After his meeting with the gods, he is condemned to roll a giant boulder up the mountainside, and just as he spies the summit, the boulder rolls back down and lands, poised and ready for him to execute the task once again. He is condemned to do it over and over with no hope of getting it over the top to the other side. This boulder doomed to roll down again for eternity.

Our Cousin Sisyphus' idea helps to develop the idea of man, who is perpetually conscious of the ultimate futility of life. Camus used the myth to show how jobs in our offices and in other futile work may cause us pain. He even suggests that to make it more bearable, one can imagine Sisyphus a happy man. I made him our cousin and gave him peripheral vision, which allows him to look from side to side, and make use of the visions as they appear. Sisyphus' job never varied. His thoughts about it, the visions and his undeniable resolve to complete his task each time, makes him somewhat of an iconic hero. One thing our hero knows is that he is free of the anxiety dealing with death. There is the eternal boulder and the eternal horizon. Any other impressions or perceptions are irrelevant to the issue."

Fields began a new page about getting old. I wondered how he knew so much about getting old when he died so young. He wrote, "The last to go is your sense of humor and your appetite. I know that aging is a universal disease, not simply local and suffered by only a few. I have watched people, as they grow older. At forty their vision has changed, at fifty they can't hear as well, at sixty they have to salt their foods to an excess, at seventy or eighty, they can't hear, see, taste, smell, or feel anything, but they can still think. Thinking is left to us at all ages, but when the ravages of age cloud and tangle your thinking, you are done."

Next is a one-page notation on the equal importance of the heart and the mind. Fields writes," How can you separate the definitions of the heart and the mind when they work together as part of the living, thinking process? When you say I love you with all of my heart, aren't you saying I love you with my mind? Doesn't the heart play the role of the mind here? Oh sure, the heart beats, pumps the blood, and is the center of physical existence, but I am talking heart and mind, as in body and soul. How do you extricate either of them? Something to think about when studying body, mind, and soul is that when you enrich the mind, you nourish the body and you uplift the soul.

So this is the deal. Just change it around and you have essentially the same thing done differently. You can enrich the body, nourish the soul and uplift the mind, or then again, you can enrich the soul, nourish the mind and uplift the body. Now you have it."

Fields talked about trade and barter as a system of economics in another part of his notebook; he said that in this way the nation would transcend the distribution and consumption issues. It would all be done individually. He said that he traded services with his barber, his friends and several university professors. He drew up plans for his favorite professor involving needed renovations to the professor's mother's home. I was not involved with this project, but I drove by it many years after the completion date.

Fields was a self-proclaimed house doctor. He helped many friends and neighbors with quality custom plans for construction to improve their homes. The plans were drawn on little sheets of paper because people back then didn't take on the fantastic mini-mansion renovations of today's homeowner. These were the trades and barters that put Fields into his chosen profession.

How well do we know one another, really? We can sleep in the same bed for over fifty years and still marvel at the things we learn about each other. The book Fields' mother gave me is still the focal point of my room. Each time I look into its pages, I see someone I knew and am getting to know better. I loved Fields; I would have done anything for him. I am able, through this book, to tell you about Fields in the intimate ways I knew him. We talked about things, but he wrote his most intimate thoughts in his journal. He seemed to take on a light filled with knowledge before his own light became extinguished.

Raphael was a well-known artist of the Renaissance period and quite popular with people during his lifetime. He was born in the late 1400's and died quite young. His paintings are very human and telling. He was exalted and worshiped by his followers. When he was suddenly taken from this world, he was mourned almost as if he were a

god, much like Fields was to me. When I saw the self-portrait Raphael painted in 1506, which hangs in a gallery in
Florence, Italy, my mind stood still. Staring sheepishly out
at me, into me, was Fields. I don't have many photos of
Fields, but this painting is very close to having a special
photo he had taken just for me.

Fields' next entry must have something to do with
the fact that he was into beginning photography. "Depth
of Fields, that's me, deep. Depth of field has something to
do with diffracted light and the zone of acceptable sharp-
ness. If light diffraction is bending the light, then it wraps
around objects, creating a lining around them. Watch the
skies and see silver linings around the clouds–diffracted
light. You want the maximum improvement in the circle
of confusion. This is the circle where you do all of the
work. You continue to increase the depth of field, and as
you increase it, it sharpens the image. I usually don't get
it right, but it makes for some good family photos. Light
is the key. Art is the light and photos are all about light.
Carefully choosing the light and its direction is the wisdom
that comes with experience. The most flattering light is
just before sunrise and just before sunset. There is a soft-

ness to it and, to get it naturally, takes perfect timing. You can simulate nature's light with photo lights brought in to back up what is missing."

On the next page he wrote, "Remember, when you use lots of exaggerated words and or expressions, you loose the effect. Avoid words like always, never, absolutely and impossible, and expressions like 'I have told you millions of times.' Some of the quotes that cause exaggerated thinking by their rhetoric are 'This is absolutely terrible and awful,' 'I cannot stand it,' 'I'll never feel better again,' and 'I am always making mistakes as I muddle through life.' As you can see, exaggerated writing produces exaggerated thinking, and exaggerated thinking leads to exaggerated feelings. Instead of negative absolutes like 'I am always unhappy,' one can be more objective and say 'I am not often as happy as I would prefer.' It is really your choice whether you think of your work and your life as an upsetting absolute or whether you choose a more objective view. Your choice is relevant to how you feel and how you feel is relevant to your choice."

There are many more pages in Fields' notebook and perhaps I will quote more someday. The very last page gives a statement that surpasses a thousand different kinds of philosophies for getting yourself in and out of perplexing situations. It says, "Make yourselves thin if the going gets mean."

I continue to open the journals, *Field Notes From Life,* containing all of the writings and notes from Fields, whenever I need his care.

Pierce's Angel

"IF YOU WANT AN ANSWER NOW, THE ANSWER IS NO; IF YOU AREWILLING TO WAIT, THEN WE CAN NEGOTIATE."

Fields had a friend named Pierce Woods who lived up in the Sierra Nevada Mountains on the central part of the eastern side of the state. They had met in the neighborhood as children and sometimes walked home from school together. Fields and Pierce strengthened their bond during these walks. I would walk with them on some occasions, but felt they had an agenda that left me out. Fields and I gave each other space during times we were with others. It felt right and fair. After Pierce moved up into the mountains they rarely saw each other, but whenever Fields visited him, he would come home full of peace.

"It's time for me to see Pierce," Fields told me.

"Yes."

"You want to go?"

He asked me to go along this time. I was hesitant, but my hesitancy gave way to desire. Not only did I want to be with Fields, but I also wanted to feel at peace.

"Yes."

A few days later, we boarded a small charter plane that looked as if it had been kept together with gum and tape. I heard creaking sounds as we climbed into our seats. The plane had four seats and two long tied-down boxes, which held supplies for fishing and mountaineering. Two men, looking very grim already occupied the two front seats. They stared straight ahead and did not acknowledge that we had come aboard.

Fields strained his neck to catch all the drama of taxiing down the short runway and taking off. I was in awe of the sights as they appeared from an elevated perspective. This was a perfect example of how familiar things changed according to how they were viewed.

I began to feel a sense of accomplishment from being up in the air. If I were an insect or a bird, I thought, I would have to beat my wings and give it all the effort in my body to gain altitude. This plane surrounding me did all the work; I sat there contemplating that I had indeed performed a feat that in past times was only a dream.

What I imagined below me were all those people who had came before me, scaling mountains, climbing glaciers, and suspending themselves over great expanses of nature. I felt an obligation to inhale all of the view at once. I was filled with both relief and apprehension—apprehension for the ascension and relief for the descent.

I had a mental task of great magnitude in my first study of perspective. I struggled to note all of the angles and how they changed the view from my new vantage point. The roaring of the plane's engine served as a hypnotic enhancer, and my mind began to grasp what my father had told me when I was younger. We were flying over the coastline of California near Monterey, and he told me that everything down there was mine. He said that I had to decide for certain what I wanted and what I was willing to do to get it. It was as if the whole world has become mine and I now had to deal with this enormous gift. I decided that I didn't want the whole world, just a tiny part of it to live my life and be comfortable.

If you look at all the things you want to attract in your life as already yours, only then can you begin to realize the meaning of "everything is or can be yours." But the kicker is, *"It's just a matter if what you are willing to do to get it."* That beachfront property you put on your wish list is already yours. What are you willing to do to get it? That car that will make you stand out in a crowd is yours, and all of the material trappings you ever dreamed of are already yours. Mental stability, the feeling of wellbeing, peace of mind, the perfect relationship, they're all yours already. The only question that arises is what are you willing to do to get them?

What an almighty relief. If it's all mine or all ours, and it's only a matter of what I am or you are willing to do for it, then, how perfectly divine. Are you willing to beat your wings with all of the effort in your body, sell your soul and die for what you want? That is up to you and certainly up to me. What a relief it is to go through the rest of your life knowing it is already yours. It gives you all sorts of secret pleasures. It frees you to make a decision about whether or not you really want it. Whether you want to put forth the effort, or put forth only the amount of effort to get the part that you want, is your choice. It is a freedom to carry with you for the rest of your wanting years.

Ever since that elevated view my father gave me of our planet, I have been rich, famous, empowered, challenged, more efficient, more effective, and all-knowing. The tensions of life lessened and I became myself, unto myself.

I had time to reflect on some more living-life truths my grandfather also gave to me via my father. A very important thing to remember is, if someone big or someone little is pressuring you for an answer, you always say, "If you want an answer now, the answer is no. If you are willing to wait, we can negotiate." Dad told me that if you say no, you can change your mind to yes, but if you say yes, you are committed to that yes and there is no way out and no way to think it over.

The next reflection revealed to me as the plane neared its destination was a saying that has held true and has mirrored events in my life. It is, "One fool offers and the other fool refuses." It will work in your life as an answer, just repeat it out loud a few times and it will become part of situations as you see them, as an explanation, and as an absolute truth.

I wanted to tell Fields of my revelations on the plane ride, but too quickly we were escorted off the plane into Pierce Woods' truck. We were on a journey and the time for personal revelations had passed, or so I thought.

The truck bounced along, the wind forced itself in through cracks in the side windows, but no one noticed because it was good to be on our way with Pierce. He stroked his long handlebar mustache, spreading the stroking to his side burns and then along the jaw line of his face. He stroked continuously as he spoke. He finally stopped the stroking, stopped the talking and sank deep into thought. After a few minutes, the stroking began again. He started to tell Fields of an unsolved disappearance in the woods just a week before we arrived. He told us that he was a prime suspect.

"Not possible," said Fields, but Pierce just shook his head while continuing the stroking and the telling of his story.

A young woman, his niece by marriage, had come

for a visit. She virtually moved into the tiny room tacked onto the side of Pierce's house. He said that the room was not in use and was in need of major repairs. Rats, squirrels and bats had taken refuge in those walls, but that his niece wasn't deterred. She set about repairing and cleaning out the old inhabitants and began to live there. She patched the windows with new panes of glass and extended the main window so that it let the sun in as rays beaming down, giving the room a heavenly quality.

The only entrance to that room and from that room into the house was through Pierce's room. According to Pierce, the girl came out rarely to take care of her living needs; most of the time she was holed up like a self-imposed hermit in the small space of that room. She was not asked to leave just as she had not been asked to stay. She didn't wander or stare into space but she did have a floating quality. It was as if she floated like an angel. Pierce said he began to call her Angel and she began to answer to that name. Her eyes were golden brown and seemed to be floating as well. Her hair was the same color as her eyes, and when she moved, her hair floated around her. She was tall and slight, and looked exactly as you would expect an angel to appear.

"That was it," he said. "She would not come into your space, she would just appear like an angel. She seemed to enjoy the moment. There was nothing before and nothing after. If you engaged her, she would be totally yours. She was illuminated as if a beam of light stayed with her. I had the feeling she plucked the moment she was with you out of the air. She gave it to you and the two of you shared it. I wondered how she was able to be so completely in the moment."

Pierce said that Angel told him she was not going to wait for a second chance to live. She had been dead and had come back to life, and did not want to be dead to life again. She said she looked at the world as if it were a dewdrop on a leaf in a cosmos on a much larger scale. She said she was part of that little dewdrop and everyone was in that dewdrop together, so why should we fret and worry about anything more than the dewdrop drying up and blowing us away.

She said that as long as the dewdrop was whole, she was going to be with it and enjoy its curative powers; she was willing to pass them on to anyone who would be in the moment with her. "I guess I loved her in a way that I knew would be brief, but I know now that she is gone that I loved her in all ways."

"Where is she?"

"She's missing. They don't have a body to consider it murder, but where else could she have gone? There is nothing for miles, just bears, some mountain lions, and other beings of the mountains. She doesn't know the mountains; not one thing does she know about survival in the wilderness. She hardly knew about surviving in a warm cozy cottage with heavenly sunbeams.

I loved her all right, and they think I may have had something to do with her disappearance. I didn't. I am her uncle, and I didn't love her the way they think. I just loved her way of living, her ideas, and I just loved her. What's wrong with loving someone?"

" Pierce, I have known you forever, and I know you didn't have anything to do with her disappearance. Is there someone I can talk with regarding knowing you for so long?"

"Let's let it be for the time being. We can talk later about it, but right now let's get settled. Fields, you can bunk with me, and Sunshine, I had you bunking with Angel. Now you will have to go it alone."

Me alone in the Sunray room made the hairs on my arms and the back of my neck bristle. I slowly pulled my bags through Pierce's room on the way to the Sunray room. I stood at the entrance to this room and observed an oasis away from all earthly presences. Sunrays filled the room. I could feel Angel all around me. I felt cold prickly fingers up and down my arms. Hugs were given to me and angel voices whispered in my ear. The voices told me I would be protected. Protected from what I wondered, but I didn't have time to think about it for long.

Smiles kept coming and going across my face. I felt loved and greeted by a strong spirit. There was love in the room, surrounding the room, but I felt no fear of the love. Yet there was something sinister, something unknown, on the edge. But I saw only the good, the loving, and the hopeful. A slightly sweet smell permeated the room. I began a shaking that could have been measured on the Richter scale as a full-fledged, major earthquake.

What happened here? Could I trust my feelings? Lay on the bed, girl, close your eyes and tell no one, the voices rasped. The voices began in the softest of tones, gathered momentum and then grew into a shouting, ear-piercing loudness. I recognized the experience as a spiritual aspect of life, widening my perspective, showing me facets of truth. There was surely a presence in the room, one that fused my mind with the unconscious suggestion that we are partners on many planes, and in this room we merge with the other side.

However absurd that seems, I lie down and fell into an extraordinarily spiritual development beyond myself. There, in that moment, I heard music and dramatizations of things I did not know. Forms manifested themselves through long corridors draped in purple and crimson velvets. Colors swirled, contributing to my subconscious mind, thinking ahead of what my conscious mind could allow.

I assumed the personality of my guide and watched as other elements became involved in a developing plot to retrieve Angel from a place amongst kindred spirits. A beat seemed to fill the room and then it was gone. My eyes opened and I was alone. I felt cleansed of bad spirits and old karma that had been residing in me for too long.

I was cleared for takeoff, but where was I going? I was determined not to leave that room. I would stay there until it was time to journey home.

Had I become Angel or had I just taken her place? There was a manifestation in this room, a presence known only to me. I needed to explore and inquire of my guide what I could do to help, or if I should wait for instructions.

"Come on, Sunshine, we're going to hunt for supper."

"Is that some kind of joke? I'm not leaving this room until I figure out what's happening in here."

"Nothing's happening here. Come on."

"I have been contacted by some voices, something wild."

"What the hell are you talking about?" Fields came into the room and looked around, hoping to find something. He looked at me, then back at Pierce's room. It was difficult, nearly impossible, for me to hide my distress from Fields; we sat on the end of the bed and talked about what had happened and the presence I felt in the Sunray room.

Fields and I agreed that spiritual moments do happen and that there are events in life we can't explain, just have to feel. He asked if I thought it was Angel trying to contact me, and, if it was, did I think I could find her. I didn't have an answer. I didn't want to go hunting, and I didn't want to be left alone. I began to feel unwell, but decided to go along on the hunt so that I would not have to face another spiritual surrender alone.

The day was bright, with rays illuminating pieces of the landscape in all directions. The forest looked motionless, yet full of vigor and energy. The melding greens and browns created a form of infusion. I could feel the forest growing inside of me, owning me, possessing me. We foraged further and found that the clearing ahead sparkled with dew. Are those the drops that Angel meant when she concluded that our universe could be just a dewdrop on a leaf in an endless parade of leaves? If so, there are many more galaxies than I had imagined.

Of course, infinity is hard for everyone to imagine. Infinity is a concept used to bring out the exploration of an existence greater than the mind can fathom. Studying and embellishing infinity is not one for reluctant brains.

It takes courage to stick with it and formulate a clear-cut concept of the phenomenon of endlessness.

I pulled myself into the clearing which was a sloping meadow ringed with ferns and soft undergrowth. I felt the same presence I had felt in Angel's room. I could hear humming. It wasn't a true humming sound; it was a calling to come forth. I followed the calling sound.

I didn't have to go far before I came upon the magical bead necklace Fields had me send to Pierce several years back. It spoke to us and led the way to finding the remains of this lovely floating angel--two piles of tiny metatarsal bones lay in two little mounds under what turned out to be two crossed legs. If these bones belonged to Pierce's Angel, then the mighty work of nature, the decomposition and renewal theory, was working overtime. The forces of the environment had left only the telltale bones of the one who previously had used them.

No one was ever accused of murder in this case; it appears that forces of nature seized Pierce's Angel. This happens in forests.

What also happened in the forest was something I will always remember.

Fields said, "Sunshine, do me a favor?"

"Sure."

"When I am gone, remember that I took you up here. Remember we saw and heard the laws of the forest. When you are teaching what you have learned, I will be a dust particle, but you can include me."

"Include you?"

"Yeah."

"What is this dust particle stuff? What do you mean 'when I am gone'?"

He never answered my question. Did he momentarily have a glance, a quick peek, into the future? I have relived those moments in the forest with Fields many times and feel the lesson he wants me to teach is the magic of the beaded necklaces, which keeps us from having to fear an encounter with a partner from another level. I have communicated with my partner, Fields, on other levels and know the joy of having experienced them.

The next day we returned to San Francisco. After Pierce reported the sighting to the authorities, the area was packed with men working on identification and taking statements from everyone in the area.

You are saying to yourself, how could there be a pile of bones after such a short while in the forest? For an answer, I command you to leave a chicken leg out in nature for a few days. You will have nothing left but the bone. The process is that swift. You haven't had the inclination to imagine the rapid demise of flesh before now, but if you have, there is no question in your mind as to the speediness at which it is consumed.

Child Of Fields

■■□ ■■

"GOOD JUDGMENT COMES FROM EXPERIENCE, AND A LOT OF
THAT COMES FROM BAD JUDGMENT."

Fields and I had what I didn't know then was some
blessed time to share in the next few weeks. He decided
to take an official leave of absence from his work in Seattle
to be closer to the unfolding events of his mother's deterioration. I was working mornings on Upper Haight and
we had every afternoon planned. Fields told me on one
of those afternoons in the park that Florrie had contacted
him with the news that she was pregnant with his child,
but that she had married another fellow and was moving
to the East Coast. She left no phone number or address,

not even her married name.

No one knew where Florrie had flown. She was carrying Fields' child. This news clutched me as if in a vise, but apparently Fields was not vise–bound. He said, "This is good news for the child."

"Won't you want to find out about this child someday?"

"No, I will let her live her life with her parents. She will be fine and won't have need of me. If she wants to know me one day, I will want to know her, not until then."

"Why do you keep calling her a her? Maybe she is a he."

"She is female and she will always be mine in blood and love. If something happens to me, Sunshine, I want you to find her someday and tell here about me."

"What would you have me say?"

"Tell her I was strong. Tell her I was a true friend, a loving son, and a damn good brother. Tell her I was handsome, if you think so, and tell her I always looked at life in a positive way, always seeing the sunshine through the clouds and rain. Tell her that I found out something a long time ago that I want her to know."

"Yes, what?"

"Tell her that the laws of nature are the same everywhere in this universe. She has to know that time and space run simultaneously, that we are sitting here and eons ago this very spot could have been underwater or a field of wild flowers, and now it is full of dwellings and organized streets, cars and inhabitants. Tell her the laws of nature she lives by today have remained the same over time, and they will not change. She should see that time and space are together in dynamics and will run together for all time. They are in symmetric balance and form the whole of the concept.

"Tell her about my inventions, and that I loved being a creator of new effects. Tell her these things for me. Tell her you love me and tell her I love you. Tell her I loved her mama once a long time ago, but time ran out on us."

"I will tell her, Fields. I will tell her," I agreed, not really thinking about anything in the future, only that at the moment he was telling me what to tell his child. At that moment, I thought Fields' face was the most beautiful face in the universe, laws or no laws. His hand clasped mine, our eyes locked, our bodies stretched out to touch from top to the toe. His heart beat in my ears as I lay my head on his chest, his blood flowed into my heart and mine into his as our love flowed together.

I have not been honest with you, but not dishonest either. Do you believe in lies by omission? This strategy of rhetoric has had me going in circles for years. I don't think the omission of a word, a letter, syllables, clauses, or unusual arrangements of words would change the context or the meaning of the intent. Drawing upon images or saying something to cause someone to come to an obvious assumption or conclusion is something we can consider, though. Those may very well be lies, but certainly not an unpardonable sin. So I have not created a sin of omission, but I have not given you accurate enough information about the intimate relationship between Fields and me. You have probably given it some thought, but let me tell you now that we had loved often and completely, and we were full of adoring passion.

Though these many years have passed and Fields has been long gone, my mind still goes to his loving me, me loving him. The first time we wholly gave ourselves physically was in the parlor of a castle-like home of a friend, according to Fields, a friend I did not know. In reality, Fields was shielding from me the fact that this was the home of a great-aunt and great-uncle; his cousin had given him the key and said, "Have a good time, buddy."

After our loving event, I walked in the dark to the powder room. I felt around for the light switch, running my hand up and down the sidewall. I was still searching for the light when a clatter of glass exploded at my feet. I felt shards of glass everywhere; I stiffened and stopped breathing. Fields ran to help, turned on the lights and put his hands around me to support my body.

My feet and lower legs were bleeding from shard assaults. I couldn't move. Fields lifted me and carried me into the main parlor. He helped me lie down on the couch. He tended to my legs, put a cool wet cloth on my forehead and set about cleaning up the thousands, probably millions, of pieces of glass from what had been glass shelving displaying vases and trinkets from worldwide travels. There, now you have heard the first of many of our intimate tales.

After we rested in the castle, which was void of occupants for an entire weekend, we slept. We slept hard and free. The next day was filled with food preparation, garden walks and a peek at the neighborhood at large. As night fell, we awoke from another long afternoon nap.

Somewhere, nowhere really, perhaps in the air dreamy music floated wistfully, music that motivated us to elevate ourselves from our sleeping places and come together in a dance. This is the dance I will always remember and no other dance will claim its place. We touched only lightly and slightly at first, then more and more as we became one entity. Our bodies moved together as if they had melted into one. The music continued to perform and we moved with it. His exhale became my inhaling and my exhaling became his breath. We moved in this state of pure wholeness for a long while; our bodies became fused and there we stayed until the crescent of the thrust and the force slowly plunging caused the magnetism to release. This special dance was our call of divinity and serenity, only to be broken by the ending of our time in the castle, and the entrance back into our own lives.

Several weeks following our castle weekend, a postcard from an east coast city announced the birth of Florrie and Field's baby girl. It arrived at the Fields' home. For many months after Fields was beaten and died, postcards continued to come from Florrie.

The flow of postcards triggered my remembering that Fields had also told me to tell his child to read Rudyard Kipling's *The Jungle Book*. In the beginning of the book, he said for her to pay particular attention to the Laws of the Jungle. He said that there are Laws of Nature and they are the truest form of life. Just like there are Laws of Nature, there are Laws of the Jungle, which are outlined in Kipling's book. The main reason places, people and things are run by laws is for survival, but laws also bring peace, harmony, and serenity to all who prevail. Man in his divine and infinite possibilities has lost touch with this fact and this direction is placed here for order as well. Fields said to tell his daughter to read the part where the Law of the Jungle never orders anything without a reason.

Fields felt strongly that his child should know about his secret to designing a successful project, no matter what it was or who requested it.

"The center is the essence," he said, "so tell her to

start there. Then she should go around the project because the circumference is the encompassing thread that
holds the essence. The essence is the heart of the project,
and enclosing the circle allows the limitations of physical
space to surface, therefore defining the project itself. It
is always so easy once you define the heart and confine it
to its own space." Child of Fields, he wanted me to tell you
these truths, as he knew them. He wanted you to know.

One true thing is that if you remember someone,
they are not dead to you. They will live in your mind
as long as you keep that memory stoked up. So we who
loved Fields and are of Fields will remember him. Carlos
Castaneda, a South American born author who wrote about
his meetings with a Yaqui Indian from Central America,
told us to watch for death; we can see it two inches to our
left at all times. Ever since I read that I have wondered if
death is waiting for us or we are waiting for it. I know now
it is there, two inches to my left. Look for it because it is
perpetually there. When I saw Fields in my mind's eye for
the last time while he was still on this earth, there was a
grievous injury to the left side of his head; death hovering
two inches to his left proved true and fatal. Once again,

I saw a flash of Tooty darting behind a nearby building, a worried look on his face.

The First Lilly

"REMEMBER THAT SILENCE IS SOMETIMES THE BEST ANSWER."

My mother was a highly critical person and nothing, I mean nothing, I did would please her. My mother's criticism bred an over-achiever. Mother had Alzheimer's disease and suffered its deterioration for fifteen years, and then Dad started the same descent. Mom was born in semi-poverty and Dad with a silver spoon in his mouth. My silver spoon needs to be polished now and then, but silver it remains. I never knew there were golden spoons until I went to the university and met many of them.

One thing that keeps me rich in focus is that I never

worry about it. Oh, I can hear you thinking, that Sunshine never had to worry about anything. She had plenty of money and a full-time maid to pick up after her, so she can talk about her rich psyche. Let me interject and tell you that a rich psyche is open and FREE to everyone. You just have to adopt it as a way to live, write the script for it in your heart, and believe it in the center of your core. A rich psyche is freedom.

My dad was a highly respected person with great wit, charm, and cleverness. He was a good father, and in the later days of his life, we became good friends.

During the years of my youth the special arrangements in my parents' household left me with a second mother. Lilly was our housekeeper for twenty-eight years. She was a staunch, fundamentalist, Church of the Nazarene member, and my parents were conservative Jews. That dichotomy added to my life, a positive element that carried me through many complicated and intricate problem resolutions. She never entered my parent's world and they never entered hers. There was a strong respect for each other's distinctions. Many ideologies were passed unassumingly by modeling; in addition to my parent's views,

Lilly's became mine.

Lilly was Marilynn's and my friend, confidante, and crucial mentor for our sanity. My parents were good parents in the respect that they wanted the best life had to offer for their children.

Many years ago, shortly after Lilly retired from her position as housekeeper for our family, she moved into a trailer court deep in the interior of the Midwest. She was near her children, and that made her happy. I went to visit Lilly, and I was happy. She showed me her pink burial dress with no pockets.

She said, "Hon, where I'm going, I won't need to take anything, so I won't be needing any pockets. Now, you make sure they bury me in this dress. I want this scarf on it and I don't want anyone looking in at me either." She was buried in her pink dress with no pockets, scarf in place, with the lid of the coffin open for all to see. I tried to get her children to close it, but that didn't happen. She looked like a skeleton, relieved of her earthly duties.

Lilly loved me like I was her own and treated me with respect, which I returned. She learned to read and write when I did. She kept our house spotless and ran around after our family catching things in mid-air. I am here to say, neither Marilynn nor I was a good housekeeper because we never quite got the dynamics of that job. Lilly brought her brand of philosophy, humor, and harmonious living to our home. I truly believe my sibling and I would both have ended up institutionalized if not for Lilly.

Lilly had her own way of disseminating her philosophy. When she wanted to get our attention and wanted us to listen, she would say, "Now you listen here, what I am going to tell you I learned from my daddy who learned it from his daddy, and they learned it from as far back as they could go, and now I'm going to tell you. You hear?"

She told us that the old ways were good ways. She spent hours explaining the old and good ways of things. In teaching us, she used all kinds of situations. She made her point, and there isn't a one of us who knew Lilly who doesn't say the very same things she used to say.

She was big on saving a little money for a rainy day. She taught us to put away our nickels, dimes, and pennies saying, "A penny saved is a penny earned." It was so simple and so true. I usually think of Lilly and something Lilly taught me every day, but especially every rainy day.

Lilly always said that you should never leave your mind idle. She said you should keep busy learning something new all of the time. She didn't think television was an important way to learn. I can hear her now.

"You can't learn nothing if you aren't doing it. You watch and you forget sooner than later. You can't leave a mind alone or someone will take it." She always said that if you leave your mind idle or unattended, someone would use it up and leave it empty. "You can't lend your mind to anybody because they don't know how to make it work best. You'd better mind your mind."

One day, when I had a problem with someone, she sat me down and said, "Don't you be a log for anyone's fire; you stay out of their way and let them burn themselves up." She had the best things to say and I wish I could remember more of her wisdom.

I don't know how a household like ours could have so much laundry, but laundry days were Monday and Thursday. My mother bought an Ironrite Automatic Mangle, Model Number 75. It was white porcelain and looked somewhat like a washing machine. She set it up in Lilly's room, and there it stayed for the next forty years.

Even after Lilly left, the mangle stood in its spot, closed and draped.

Lilly would do the laundry in the washing machine, dry it in the dryer and put the finishing touches on everything using that mangle ironer. I can see her now sitting in front of that machine with her hands flying over it. I can smell the fresh scent of the finished pieces as they came off that mangle. She would fold and place each piece on her bed as if it were a piece of couture designer apparel.

Lilly made homemade lemon meringue pie and fried chicken that I can still smell and taste all these years later. I have never tasted a lemon meringue pie or fried chicken to equal it. I have looked for Lilly's lemon meringue pie. I have tried many a fried chicken meal. I have always been sadly disappointed because nothing has ever equaled those Lilly-made meals.

Lilly would always make extra fried chicken because she wanted us to have leftover snacks. Now that I think of it, we would go to the refrigerator several times on fried chicken nights. Since Lilly's room was right off the kitchen, she would hear us and come out to see our delight. We would sit at the kitchen table and talk, or I should say

Lilly would talk and we listened as we downed a second and third piece of chicken. I think we learned about life and how to handle many things from those leftover fried chicken talks with Lilly.

Everyday at two-thirty in the afternoon, Lilly closed her door, pulled down the blinds and took a twenty-minute nap. She said she was sure that a person who napped every day for ten to twenty minutes lived longer, way longer than those who did not. She was not a scientist with research data to prove how she felt, but she had seen enough folks come and go on this earth to have firsthand observations on which to base her conclusions.

Lilly knew everyone in the neighborhood and they sought her advice on just about everything. Her magical moral view of life was connected to her childhood training, her very devout views of heaven and hell, and the teachings of God.

Florrie knew about our love and respect for Lilly. When she found out she was pregnant, she didn't know what to do or how to deal with the child inside her; she came to visit and talk with Lilly. I didn't know it at the time, but many people came to talk with Lilly and seek her golden advice. Lilly had her own trademark when it came to decision-making and living your life morally according to God's wishes.

Florrie and Lilly worked it through together. After soul-searching on Florrie's part and teaching of values on Lilly's, it was decided the child would stay in Florrie's belly and grow to maturation. But the story doesn't end there. The teachings of our Lilly went on into the next generation. Florrie named Fields' child Lilly as a remembrance, to pay respect, and to repay the debt of life Lilly had given. The life that would carry Fields into the next generation, his child, Lilly.

As the years passed, the advent of the Internet finally reached my corner of the world. One day I thought to myself I would just type in Florenzia Sharpay. In a flash, several pages popped on the screen. I quickly learned that Florenzia was an editorial project manager for an award-winning weekly magazine featuring announcements and book reviews of literary works. She had a number of publications in her own right. Was this Fields' Florrie, the mother of his child? Was this the right thing for me to pursue? What would I gain from this endeavor? Fields' daughter would be practically middle-aged now. What was I doing? As I scanned the screen in indecision, I noticed a tiny box on the magazine Web page that stated, contact us. Someone told me long ago, "Let sleeping dogs lie." So I did.

A Meeting

◻◼◻ ◼◻

*"IF YOU FIND YOURSELF IN A HOLE, THE FIRST THING
TO DO IS STOP DIGGING."*

After Fields passed and I moved to Los Angeles, times changed, ideas changed, our old neighborhood changed; the revolution of flowers and peace took over. People a few years younger than us flooded the streets, dressed in loose clothing and centering their activities in the Haight-Ashbury District where we grew up. Fields changed into a gravesite and I became an Angelino.

Florrie was sixty, considering retirement, and her daughter Lilly, by Fields, was forty when someone who was best friends with Florrie contacted me. She identified her-

self as Star Hershing.   She had known Florrie and Fields
when they were together.   She was their good friend; I
remember her well from those past years.   She began our
conversation with some personal information that fueled
an ember waiting for a time to flare up and ignite my wild-
est dreams.

Star and I met in the cafeteria at Nordstrom's new
department store. We recognized each other by the red
sweaters we decided ahead of time to wear for identification purposes.   Star walked with a cane and said that
she suffered from an autoimmune disease.   I neglected
to pursue the subject and hear the descriptions of her af-
flictions. We both had come for a purpose and it wasn't
friendship. I wondered in the days following our meeting
why we didn't gather friendship out of the meeting; we
chattered and enjoyed each other's company as if we were
long-lost sisters meeting again for the first time in forty
years. Yet friendship was not the agenda.

Star said, "The years have certainly gone by, haven't
they?"

I said, "Yes, that's for sure."

"It was so very sad for all of us when Fields passed

so young. I knew him only through Florrie, but you knew him so well when you were kids."

"I loved him so much." I said.

"I know you did and Florrie wanted me to tell you that she appreciated your being good to her."

I thought about it and then decided to ask," I know you and Florrie were best friends, so maybe you know why she didn't talk to Fields about the baby coming?"

"She told me she didn't say anything to him because she did not think she was going to go through with it and have his baby. She knew they weren't going to last. They both knew it. She thought it would be easier if Fields didn't know about the baby; she decided to handle it herself."

Then Star got to the point of our meeting. "Florrie and Lilly will be in San Francisco next month for a visit. I want your permission to talk to them about you. I want to set up a meeting for all of you. I want to give Florrie time to tell Lilly things she needs to tell her before the meeting. I know both of them will want to meet with you. I know you have things to tell them that will add an important dimension to their lives."

"That would be remarkable. I'd like that."

Star gave me Florrie's phone number and said, "I'll call Florrie and tell her you are going to call her and make the arrangements for the meeting."

"Fine, I'll do that."

My mind wandered as I sipped my tea. I imagined meeting Florrie and Lilly as if it were already taking place. I know we will visit the old neighborhood and nothing will be the same. We will walk in the park and look at the city. We will visit Fields in his final resting place and say kind, tearful words to him. Will he see his child? If the spirit or any part of the soul remains at the gravesite, he will be there, and he will see her.

Florrie and Lilly and I will have dinner and talk of times past. I will hear what Lilly is willing to say to me. I want to ask her questions and I expect she will have answers. I would like to hear Florrie's life story, as she believes it to be. Would she tell me all of the good things? Will I hear about her successful husband Glenn? Will I hear about her children and grandchildren? Will I hear she is happy?

I will tell them that Fields' mother drowned in the

bathtub many years ago while his aunt was making dinner. Auntie never recovered from that loss during her watch. I wonder, will I tell Lilly and Florrie that I am happy? Yes, I am happy, I will tell them.

I knew I wouldn't tell them of the time Fields and I went hiking in the mountains. It was a gloriously sunny day and he kept calling me Sunny. He was the only person in my whole lifetime who ever called me Sunny. I always wondered whether anyone would again.

I envision that during our meeting I will tell Florrie and Lilly about Fields' funeral, how the day was bleak and rainy. There wasn't a dry eye or a dry boot in the group of friends and family who had gathered to say goodbye to Fields. I would tell them that Fields' mother, Eugenia, and his brother Brock, stood silently throughout the service and the walk to the gravesite. Tears clouded their vision but they cried in private. I will tell them the service on that day revealed that Fields had been of great value to his family, his friends, his firm, and, unbeknownst to all us, his legacy.

We will spend the afternoon relating stories about Fields that will bring him alive and make his memory meaningful to Lilly. We will give her the missing pieces so that she can continue to build herself into the new picture. She will have pieces of Fields to include in her continuing self-discovery.

I will end the day with some of the philosophies Fields gathered from one of his favorite childhood books, *The Little Prince.* I will tell Lilly that Fields never liked to have guests pop in unannounced. You always had to announce your arrival with time to spare. Fields said that if you popped in on him, he would not have time to prepare his heart for your visit. He needed time to think about being together. He felt that sharing time together was a special, intimate experience and he should be prepared for it ahead of the moment. He said that visits and sharing moments were not to be hurried into or out of, but that they were to be cherished and planned with your heart and mind prepared.

One of Fields' favorite answers was, "Give it some time." I will tell Florrie and Lilly that we should think about what Fields was telling us because it would hold true time and time again. It will ring true every time they thought about sharing time with someone and taking time to prepare for the moment. Fields will live in their hearts as he lives in mine. I will give them time.

I will give Lilly the journal, *Field Notes* that her father wrote over forty-five years ago. I will show her my favorite parts; I will tell her how hard it is for me to part with it, but that it is in the right hands. She now will have information to share with her children and they will begin to learn about and to know someone they did not realize was connected so deeply and permanently to them.

I want Lilly to know that the journal Fields wrote is the only concrete physical evidence of his being, besides the living evidence of his life. I want her to know that as she reads this journal and understands her father's internal dreams, that this book and its contents is only a peep into the man I knew.

There is a special part of the journal that I love because it stands out as something I never thought Fields would, or could, write. On a page toward the middle of Fields' journal, he says, "No one knows this, but Cinderella is Jewish and the prince is Catholic. They never got together, as the story states, because the shoe fit another maiden and they each married someone else.

Cinderella ran away from the wicked stepmother and evil sisters, but not before she told me she was working on a play. This is the play he wrote.

<u>Scene Opens</u>

"My sisters are cross with me, and when they are cross, they are mean little suckers. The fact that my most creative work is done in the nude pisses them off. I sweep out that chimney lickety split and I know if it weren't for me, it would be–it should be them."

"Cindy, you are ordered to sweep three more chimneys and you know all the neighbors want their work done. Now get to it."

"Yeah, I will."

"Cindy, help me zip up this dress."

"Fix this trim."

"Put my hair in curls."

"Hurry, we'll be late."

<u>Enter The Fairy Godmother</u>

"Hello, darlin'? How are things going with you here in horror land?"

"The usual. What's happening?"

"El Prinzo is giving a ball tonight and he is looking

for a bride. Do you want to go, darlin'?"

"Sure do, but Fairy Godmother, what shall I wear?"

"No problem for a Fairy Godmother." With one wave of the wand, there stands Cindy. looking like a princess.

"How is that?"

"Looking good, but Fairy Godmother, can you please make my sisters Mamaka, Mousieypoo, Monkeykins, and little Duckydoo nude for this special occasion? It would make me so happy, and I will never ask anything of you again, I promise."

"Darlin, the moment you arrive in your coach, they will be nude, but remember, you must run from the ball at exactly twelve midnight."

"Oh, I know that, Fairy Godmother. I surely do know that."

"Goodbye, Cindy. I must go on but I have planned for you to meet a handsome son of the butcher in a village far, far from here. You will be happy and have many children to keep you company in your old age; meanwhile, get this prince and the ball thing done and out of the way so we can go on with the story."

Enter Cindy

The ball is in progress and it looks like Mamaka, Mouseypoo, Monkeykins and Duckydoo are having a marvelous time. They stop dead in their tracks when they see Cindy dressed like a real princess. They shriek in horror as their dresses and undergarments drift off of them into the air and out the palace doors.

The rest of the story is history. Cindy runs away at the strike of twelve, looses her shoe, which becomes fitted the next day with the wrong girl. Years later, Cindy can be seen frolicking with her six children on the hills and in the dales of a village far, far away from the wicked life she left.

An Alternative Ending:

Everyone sheds their clothes at the ball and Cindy and the prince elope to live as nudists happily ever after.

The End

This was exactly Fields. This was fun to him. I gather that the point of this story was the importance of choice. He always weighed his choices with lists for pro and con. He wrote out rewards and consequences. I remember that decisions came hard for him.

After the play, Fields added another piece at the end of the play where he defined the word *"word."* "He posed the question, "What is a word? A word is a visual thought. What are words when they are strung out in a line with a period at the end? A sentence. Then, a sentence is incorporated into a paragraph, ultimately into pages of visual thoughts for your pleasure and or pain."

Fields continued on page after wonderful page. He wrote, "You can get into a study of Heuristics, which I gather, is the nature of solutions of space. How would you solve a packing problem? Would you choose the biggest item first, filling in the cracks later? Put all of the little items on the top or bottom, or choose a separate box altogether? Rather than make a total decision, would you be better able to solve the problem in small steps, by changing the values and the techniques.

"Scheduling problems can be a time/space relationship, needing Hyperheuristics for scheduling. The goal should be to minimize the time lags and maximize the investment of time. You can use this approach to solve personal scheduling problems and leave yourself in a white or a non-white space, according to how you gain the required techniques of solving the time/space relationship."

Fields was a simple fellow on the outside, but his interests were vast and varied. I did not know that he got to the total depths of anything much but he certainly liked to scurry around in a curious haste. I think his haste stemmed from an internal notion that his clock had fewer tics than most.

Fields got into cowboy stuff for a while and wore the shirts with mother-of-pearl snaps and a sewn-in dipped point in the back. Most of them were plaid, either blue or brown. He wore a big ten-gallon hat and started spouting sayings he collected in his journal. He said the most favorite in his collection was, "Always drink upstream from the herd."

I tend to agree with Fields, that you better drink upstream. He had lists and lists of quotes of cowboy wisdom, and from the curls at the ends of his journal's pages, it shows he has read and reread them. Some of his collected sayings are included at the beginnings of each chapter of this accounting of Fields' and my life together. I do not know who the original authors were, but many of these sayings can be attributed to Mark Twain and Will Rogers.

Fields would be pleased to know that I have shared them with you.

Fields started his last journal entry with a quote that I think is his own original point of view, "I started the day thinking I was really something bigger than big itself. Strolling along in my self-contained way, I probably should have recognized I was feeling too good."

He then wrote, "I know I am a city boy, born and bred, but this cowboy thing really interests me. I read up on some ranches in Oklahoma and I thought about going out there and seeing if I could get along. I spoke with some guys at Casey's Bar, and they said that life is hard for cowboys. I think cowboys are the epitome of masculinity. They are, and mostly they have to work at it. They look after all the needs of the cattle--feeding, branding, repairing fences, and, best of all, they ride on the backs of horses. I thought riding horses was the thing I liked most, until I spent a whole day riding out in the country. I'm beginning to think my Wild Bill Hickock/Lone Ranger (my favorite)/Buffalo Bill/Jesse James/Wyatt Earp days are under the saddle. I still like some of the sayings I heard at Casey's. Here's a good one for you: 'Your fences need to be horse-high, pig-tight and bull-strong.'"

After my meeting with Florrie and Lilly, I plan to leave this journal I have enjoyed all of these years since Fields left us in the hands of his daughter. I love thinking that he will be so happy that she will share ideas from the father she never knew and tell her children about their grandfather, Fletcher Fields.

Florrie

"IF YOU ARE RIDING THE HERD, TAKE A LOOK BACK EVERY NOW AND THEN TO MAKE SURE IT'S STILL THERE WITH YOU."

What happened in 1962? Lilly, child of Fields, was born on a summer evening when the balm of the night was at its peak. She slid into this world, a perfectly beautiful specimen of the reproductive process. Mother and child were doing well.

Florrie told me her life had changed quickly. She met and married Stanford Sharpay, and moved away. Florrie said that after Lilly's birth, something snapped in her; she flew the coop, leaving Lilly with Sharpay.

In what felt like an instant to her, Florrie was back;

she was back before Lilly was speaking in complete sentences. Life picked up as usual and nothing was ever mentioned about the break in that household again.

Florrie said that Stanford Sharpay had been brought
up in a small town in Kentucky. His mother was a pre-
school teacher and his father was a rather famous tender
of horses. Stanford's dad was the original horse whisperer.
He could talk to horses and always got the horses to talk
back to him. Florrie said it was quite interesting to watch.
Stanford watched for many hours, but he never quite figured out the secret of horse whispering. He was always
treated as a special child because of his birth limp. Florrie
felt that if anything could have been done, the Sharpays
would have done it, but all his parents ever did was buy
him special shoes that eased his pain and elevated the
shorter leg to nearly match the length of his other leg.

Florrie told me she learned about her own brilliance
in the brief time she was away from Lilly and Stanford.
She became aware of others. She learned a style of living
she never could have imagined. She learned to dance
and throw her arms up and turn her face to the sun and
the wind in great abandonment. She picked flowers in

fields and thought of her past, her present and her future all in the same flashing instant. She educated herself by teaching others how to get the most out of each moment. She knew the life she was leading was as deep and as wide as she was ever going to live again, and time clamped its creeping hands upon her shoulders and pulled her home to her baby and her husband who was waiting patiently as a saint. Lilly and her Saint Stanford were there to greet her return.

Florrie will tell you, as she told me, that she would always remember her brief life living in the present. It is a remembrance that will carry her to the end of her days. It is a part of the life she now shares with Lilly.

I envisioned Florrie telling Lilly about Fields. Of course, she couldn't tell her the things I remember or the way I remembered them. She could never tell Lilly how much I loved Fields, nor would I. Lilly will have to find out that loving Fields would never take from her what she has now; it would only add to her life in a gentle and tender way.

If Fields were alive, he would share many more moments with Lilly, but in his state he will have to rely on those who loved him to impart his essence and peeks into his journal to explain and validate his existence.

Florrie told me that she and her husband, Saint Stanford, continued their lives together and produced five more offspring.   Lilly and her brothers and sisters looked similar in many ways; neither the outside world nor their inside world expressed any doubt, that they all belonged to each other.

Florrie did not tell Lilly about her father, Fletcher Fields, until I contacted them about the meeting set up by Star Hershing. I imagined the telling broke Lilly's world apart, and her mind struggling to determine what was really true and what her new blood line would reveal. I imagined her breaking down in sobs and barely able to get out the questions she had for Florrie.

I pictured Florrie, on the other hand, stammering and stuttering to give the details to Lilly whom she loved with such a fury. Florrie loved all of her children with the same fierceness but, when trouble or difficulties plagued one, she would intensify her ferocious love for that one in particular.

Florrie said that her task of telling Lilly about

Fields didn't come easily and didn't flow. It came in spits and spurts. It came burping out of her mouth and her memory like unwanted air in the pipes. She told her as much as she wanted her to know and much less than she remembered.

I wanted to know what Lilly knew about Fields, all she knew. Did she know that he loved Saturday mornings because he did not have to shave? Did she know that he hated the cold of ice cream on his teeth and loved peanut butter cookies? Did she know that he wrote in his journal, loved walking in the park, feeding the ducks, telling lies to his sister and making her cry? Did she know that Fields felt he was most like a humming bird? He thought that the swift beating of their wings mirrored what he felt like inside. He said that they were using up their lives too quickly and that they would be dead too quickly, sometimes within hours of when we saw them flitting around the honeysuckle bushes.

Did Lilly know that he cared about looking perfect in front of others? His mother told me he didn't crawl in public, but would practice privately, and then, one day he crawled out in the open. She said he didn't practice walking by pulling up on the tables, and then tumbling back down, in public. He practiced walking privately. One day he just walked out of his private practice room and never tumbled in front of anyone. Fields always practiced everything in private; you never saw him doing anything until he did it like an expert.

Lilly

"DON'T INTERFERE WITH SOMETHING THAT ISN'T BOTHERING YOU."

Lilly and I met in San Francisco several times in the following years to share with each other many of our innermost secrets and to visit Fields' final resting place. I discovered quickly that Lilly, child of Fields, did not seem like a fragile woman, but could split apart at the seams for simple reasons. She was an emotionally charged lady looking for love and kindness, and she took it however it came. It usually came in unlikely forms. It came in the form of having seven babies and finding motherhood a daunting task, with love flooding out but not circling back.

Lilly told me about the contradictions in her, about how words to the music kept telling her, teaching her, and melodiously lulling her away from the moral teachings of her upbringing and into a creative, rebellious state. But why did she seek out friends who were critical and pessimistic? They curbed her creativity and her outward search for a reality within of herself.

Before her marriage to Lt. Marion Brady, M.D., and the arrival of her children, pot and LSD numbed and cancelled her desire to soar within boundaries set by society. In history lessons, she learned about the bombings during World War II, the invasion of other countries, the Kennedy's, and Dr. Martin Luther King, Jr. When her teacher said, "There are hundreds of wars going on right now as we sit in this classroom, and hundreds of people are dying because of those wars," Lilly bolted from the room because of her sensitivity, and was determined to live a fuller life by helping others in need. She was young then, and did not learn until years later of her own desperate need to be helped.

Lilly learned to write well by taking an Advanced English class. Every day the teacher would write another topic on the board. She gave the class 40 minutes to write their compositions on the day's topic. When the teacher tinkled her car key against her glass, each student would pass his or her paper to the left. When she tinkled the key against her glass again, each student started reading the paper currently in hand and then graded it. Graded papers were then returned to their owners. The teacher would call each name and record the grade the paper had received.

Invariably, Lilly's paper would fall into the hands of the most exquisite male human being she had ever beheld, Gary. She so wanted him to love her work. Each and every time he would read her paper, he would give her a B, a B-, or a B+, but never ever an A or even an A-. Lilly claimed that this English class, with the tinkling bell and the handsome judgmental human being, shaped her into someone who was constantly seeking approval from exquisitely handsome human beings and always feeling her work is less than an A.

Of course, it is not nearly as simple as the English compositions and societal violence; it was Lilly's need for approval that drove her to join the Peace Corps. She saw it as a way to help the world. The ten countries offered to her were India, Nepal, Peru, Ghana, Kenya, Costa Rica, Tanzania, Thailand, Brazil and China. Lilly chose to work in an orphanage in Nepal, which seemed best suited to her goals.

The orphanage project allowed her to sleep with the children and practice learning the language. She was able to give outwardly and, most importantly, nourish her psyche by giving and getting love and passion from the children in that orphanage. She ended up being an English teacher and sharing her culture with her charges.

Lilly signed up for a twelve-week program, which she thought would give her time to acclimate and immerse her self in the Nepalese culture and lifestyle. Many of the children had health problems. As the volunteer in charge of their wellbeing, Lilly had contact with volunteer medical personnel as well. This is how she met her husband-to-be.

The variety of experiences Lilly acquired in her teen and young adult years did something for her that no one person and no one single experience could have done. As she kept working, her bank account kept growing, but so did her needs. One thing Lilly had learned along the way, though, was to be a good money manager. After a number of years and a lot of good management, Lilly realized that she was not using all of her savings. Her interest in charitable organizations began to grow. She volunteered for some of the charities to study how they worked, if they worked, and how they were organized.

Lilly felt it was important for her to give back to the world some of what she had taken. She financed a public charity called American/Global Trust, an organization founded with one thousand dollars from her savings. Its mission is to share ethical standards worldwide, care for children in need and educate them, promote civil and human rights and celebrate diversity in our world.

It sounded to me like a big task, but in reality Lilly currently explains in her global speeches that this work remains a special service to meet human needs. She shows how environmental and social issues tie in with health innovations. She explains that using responsibility and technology solutions insure that they all weave into each other and become one entity.

Her charitable organization has been in existence for 23 years now and has many major business and industry supporters, including the movie industry. She continues to play the leadership role in this charity, but has hired professionals to run the charitable events and drives that are held several times a year.

Last year, Lilly and her family traveled to Washington, D.C., to receive an award from the President of the United States for her extraordinary work. Lilly never talks about her work with her charity when we meet. I found out about it from Florrie, who carries on an extensive e-mail correspondence with me to this day.

When I first met Lilly, I could not believe how she resembled Fields. I could not have painted a more perfect replica of Fields. Her nose is the same. Her eyes are bigger, wider apart, and feminine. The have the same dark, almost black, squinting all-knowing look in them. Lilly's head tilts to the left, as did Fields'. Lilly is left-handed, as was Fields.

The tilt is the important resemblance. Fields showed how he was feeling by the angle and the depth of his tilt. When Lilly smiles I see Fields again. I see the soft smiling lines positioned in exactly the same places on each of their faces. Her eyes tell stories without uttering a single word, just as Fields' eyes told his stories. Her nose is that of Raphael's self-portrait. When I first looked at her, I saw that her front left tooth was a bit jagged and raised, slightly flapping over the tooth beside it, making for her endearing smile. Fields' front tooth had been shaped the same way. It was easy to see that Fields left his mark physically on Lilly. I didn't tell her what I saw.

What will Lilly tell her children about our Fields? After she hears about all the love from those of us who knew him, will she love him, too? Will she tell her children about their grandfather, Fletcher Fields? Will she study his journal and learn what he was thinking and then share that with them? Will she understand what I understand, what Florrie understands? She will not but she will give her children the chance to know him in their own way.

Lilly's Children, Fields' Grandchildren

■■■■■

*"GOD GAVE ME MY TALENT, AND I WAS AFRAID OF FACING HIM
ONE DAY IF I DIDN'T USE IT."*

Dr. and Mrs. Marion Brady sent out birth announcements for each of their seven children. According to Lilly, each was treated like a new miracle, treasured and cherished as a prized gift. Each was an individual, given every opportunity to thrive, flourish, and bloom into First In Show.

The first child to arrive came into this world three weeks earlier than scheduled. The doctor told the Brady's that a child comes into this world when he or she is ready and this one was perfectly ready, right at his own time.

Louis Charles Brady will someday make his parents proud of him as a son and as a friend. Louis became everyone's friend. Everyone admires him for many different reasons, as many reasons friends have for admiring each other. Louis learned that to make and keep friends, first you had to be one, and he was always good at that.

The second child to arrive in the Brady clan came expectedly on the exact scheduled day of arrival. Mira Clara Brady arrived at 7:34 P.M. on July 4th, amid the sounds of a nearby fireworks display. She was properly announced and grew to be as loud as the firecrackers that had announced her arrival. She could be heard for miles; listen, you can hear her now. She has an ego disorder that commands everyone's attention even before she comes into full view. Her heart is made of pure gold, and she has diamonds surrounding her soul.

The third child was born during a political crisis. Once, for a school report, Michael Morris Brady gave an oral and written report on the events surrounding the days before and after his birth. He presented it in a way that was spellbinding, just like all of his stories and plays. Many of his plays have been performed on stage. Michael is like a spider, weaving webs of intrigue with depressed and desperate plots. His name is up in lights; he has a brilliant future.

The fourth child to enter the Brady family came out wailing, flailing, and flapping. She has not stopped yet. Margaret "Marty" Rose Brady is a lovely young lady and very accomplished. She is the image of her mother in looks and the exact opposite in personality. Lilly confessed that she has tried to bring Marty into her charity work, but the complaining grunts and groans encouraged Lilly to let Marty Rose go her own way. Lilly says that when you see her with her gang of friends, you see they are all exactly the same in temperament. They perfectly illustrate the saying, "birds of a feather."

Number five is alive--barely. Justin Peter Brady arrived at 11:59 p.m. on December 31st. He was a New Year's Eve baby, as close to the New Year as he could get. Peter, called by his middle name, has spent his life missing everything by a second, a moment, a day, a month, but missing them all the same. You would imagine that he would spend his time deeply depressed as a result of this but he is happy in spite of his missed connections. He looks at living differently from others in his family, maybe differently from anyone in the universe. His disconnections leave room for reconnections and reasons for reconnections govern his life. Peter Brady is a happy person whose life does not work on time but works on universal elements working together to formulate his existence.

Florrie's unspoken favorite, Lilly's sixth child, Faye Ray Brady, came in conjunction with a ray of light that beamed down on the spot where she was born. She came so quickly into the world that her mother barely realized the process of birth had begun until it was finished. Faye Ray continues to spend her life finished before the process has actually begun. This has allowed her to never start anything, never have to commit at the beginning so never having realize an end. She is simply a Johnny-come-lately flower child. She is in her own right time and in her own right place.

Florrie has spent many thousands of hours and tens of thousands of dollars on a therapeutic cure for Faye Ray, never seeing a difference for all her efforts. Many a kind soul begins things for Faye, helping her along until the end, thus seeing her through the process. Once finished,

Faye Ray says a kind thank you or two and then continues starting nothing, enjoying everything.

Sons are prayed for, ritualized and revered, as was the case with child number seven, lucky number seven, who was presented in the breech position. James Nathan Brady always and forevermore presents feet first. You have to watch his oversized feet because they are always in the way, coming in first, stumbling over each other, one a size larger than the other, making their owner famous for his peculiar, quite large feet. According to Lilly, James has never felt worthy of the love and praise, always bestowed upon him. His heart breaks because he cannot return love. It stays in his heart and sticks in his throat. As the years pass, hopefully, he will gain breakthrough status and become all that his legacy predicts.

I quizzed Lilly carefully about her life and her children's lives over the many times we met because they are directly connected to Fields. Inside of Lilly, inside her children and their children, lie drops of Fields. They will continue to pass his kernel of reality on as it was passed on to him. We are unacquainted with the conceivable opportunities and the expectations presented through this line of Field's family. However as they make their way, taking paths known and unknown, rough or silky, clear or obscure, they will be comforted by each other, and those drops of Fields will be the magisterial characteristic that determines their inevitabilities.

Aunt Eugenia's Children
■■■ ■■

"IT'S BETTER TO BE A HAS-BEEN THAN A NEVER-WAS."

I learned about Eugenia and her children after we reconnected. She is the only sister of Fields. She became a teacher, an administrator and, eventually, an important board of education member from her district. She was elected to office and was stalwartly supported in her efforts to improve the district's system from the ground up. She was quite innovative and managed to formulate many changes. She married Mr. Gerard Bloomings, a city councilman, first and foremost because she loved him but also because he was calm and quiet, a settled-in sort of guy, busy with his own rather demanding career. This type of husband gave Eugenia an opportunity to do the things she wanted and needed to do in relative peace, without lengthy explanations.

She raised their three children. She enrolled them in excellent schools and studied how to give these next-generation neophytes, skills that would keep them in the forefront of society and would give them what she considered necessary to catch the golden ring. Mr. Bloomings' silence during the raising of his children stemmed from his fear of Eugenia.

During the ensuing years, I kept contact with Eugenia. We spoke by phone now and again, visited on those rare occasions when I returned to San Francisco, and shared reminiscences of Fields. Eugenia was always open, but kept her family isolated from many outside influences, past and present.

As a young woman, Eugenia was a towering beauty, letting her wavy mane hang free to bounce and twist with her every movement. If you were to follow behind her at some distance, you would see nearly every man, woman, and child she passed turn to get another look at this movement of beauty.

Eugenia was a good neighbor and was acknowledged for it. She organized the first Neighborhood Watch Program, sought and won legislation to build a park on land that had been designated for it years before the neighborhood grew up around it. She welcomed new neighbors as well as helped her neighbors in need. She did the little things like pick up a child when the parents had commitments that conflicted with their schedules for picking up, plus she did big things like stay all night with a frightened and lonely neighbor. More awards followed in Eugenia's life, but to her way of thinking, the Good Neighbor Award stood out as her single most important accomplishment. Remember Eugenia's talents; remember her pride and her professionalism. Also remember her neighborliness; remember her enduring love for her husband Gerard. Remember her love for her brother and remember her love for her children.

After a lifetime of loving and giving, Eugenia's life is now vacant, barren and forlorn. She spends her days roaming around from store to store, and from her mother's house to her own house. The Mom's house is as vacant as Eugenia's life. Gerard is now gone; perhaps he has met Fields in that place beyond what we know.

The innovations and the many changes Eugenia was able to make remain only as memories. Her Good Neighbor Award hangs in her room above the bed. She never looks at it because it has become part of the setting and has melted into everything else. There is no one who remembers Eugenia and her professional life, her motherhood, her elected positions, and no one remembers Gerard. He died and left her.

Eugenia's hair is white, her skin is white, the whites of her eyes are red, her teeth are yellow and her smile has faded into a permanent sneer. Her wanderings have begun to worry her children, Fletch, Fleming, and Felicia. Fletcher is the first-born and the name she gave him signaled Eugenia's desire to recapture something of her brother, Fields.

Fletcher Bloomings is so far from what she expected and hoped for. His frame is square and squat; his head is flat at the back. He has slightly olive skin and lids that hood his brown eyes, which are set too close together. His lips look as if he has just come from monthly collagen injections. His personality is exactly what you would not have imagined from sweet, good-natured, good neighbor Eugenia. Fletcher is meaner than a junkyard dog.

He is well educated and is well positioned in a law firm where he has monthly parking fees, a glassed-in corner office and several secretaries; he answers to virtually no one. He never married and is content to buy his love. Fletcher is a drug addict. He has been in and out of rehab centers and is nearly hopeless. He is lucky to have been able to keep his position and has done so only because he has a strong will and tempers himself enough to survive the real world and soar on the other side of his life. He does not see his mother because he thinks he doesn't have the time. He does not contact his sister or brother because he feels he has in some ways grown above them and has grown beyond them. They would have nothing to talk about. He does not have a wife or friends, and he doesn't want or think he deserves them. Though he is a part of Eugenia's hope for the future; it did not happen.

The twins, Fleming and Felicia are not close but they maintain a relationship with each other and their respective families that is quite acceptable. Each thinks the other is selfish and self-centered; they have constant altercations that stem from each asking the other for a favor. When the favor or the errand is not granted due to constraints on one or the other, an eruption gets into full swing. Each argument lasts for varying periods of time, and always resolves after some time has passed.

Fleming is tall, quite different from Fletcher, the opposite of Fields. His hair is light brown, not distinctive, but still attractive. His face shows the calmness of his father, the peacefulness of his mother, and, I believe, the love of Fields. His smile is distinctively characteristic of a person who does not hold back. His eyes glimmer and flash, and you know that he is a caring person. He doesn't laugh out loud, ever, but his smile is always readily and given.

Fleming married the mayor's daughter, and they remain childless. His wife, Niva, is Eugenia's only advocate because she acknowledges her love and checks to maintain her comfort. Fleming was creative as were all his friends: the juggler, the slack ropewalker, the body contortionists, the clown, acrobats, aerialists, magicians, mime artists, and storytellers. The kids in the park loved to watch the developing performances.

Fleming created and organized a circus, not like the Ringling Brothers with animals, high wires and tents, but a small version with performances held nightly in the San Francisco area. Soon, they were performing in several cities on the West Coast and moving eastward. His passionate circus fervor lasted only a few years.

Next, he found his niche as a sports broadcaster for a small television company along the Central Coast. His union with lovely, sweet, Niva has produced no children and Eugenia waits. She, more than Fleming, hoped they would have a son. Somehow Eugenia was looking secretly for Fields in her own offspring, but openly hoping for him to return to her through her grandchildren.

Felicia died way too young. What happened to Felicia was everyone's comment at the funeral. During the funeral, Eugenia's eyes never opened and she never uttered a word. She explained to me later that Felicia found herself in bad company, and hung out with the wrong sort. She was found dead in a motel room, which doubled as a methamphetamine laboratory. All of the inhabitants of the room had inhaled poisonous gasses and died during that night. The story did not hit the news until after the funeral, which made the day of burial calmer. When the news did come out, it went unnoticed except by the family and a few neighborhood friends.

Eugenia was never the same after Felicia's untimely death. Her voice lowered to a whisper, her eyes were always at half-mast, and her hair was knotted and close to her head. Her lips developed a tremor and are never motionless.

A rather lengthy magazine article came out about methamphetamine labs and their growing numbers in the Bay Area. The ring of entrepreneurs, of which Felicia was a part, and their demise were spelled out in a clear picture. The article eventually came to Florrie and Lilly's attention and they talked at length about Fields, Eugenia, and the family ties to Lilly.

It was Lilly who wanted to contact Eugenia because Eugenia is, after all, her aunt. For so many years, Eugenia and her children were unknown to Lilly; now she wanted to make up for the time she was disconnected from what belonged to her. Fields' blood and Fields' bones make this her ancestral circle.

Lilly's phone call came early one evening as the rain beat down upon the little neighborhood house; that first ring seemed to bring the darkened house back to life. Eugenia sat, as she often did, in triumphant amusement at her ability to sit alone, day after night, day again, alone in an environment she has created to mirror her loneliness. The phone rang many times before she summoned the strength to pick up the receiver and utter, "Hello."

"Hello, Eugenia?"

"Yes, this is Eugenia."

"My name is Lilly; I am your niece."

"No, dear, you are certainly mistaken because I am no one's aunt."

"I know this is hard for you. It is hard for me, but you are my aunt."

"How did you get my number? I think you have the wrong Eugenia; you see, I am Eugenia Fields-Bloomings."

"I think you are the right Eugenia. You had a brother named Fletcher Fields, right?"

A burst of recognition and a slideshow of Fields came bursting into her mind. She was unable to answer.

"I am Lilly, My father was Fletcher Fields and my

mother is Florrie Sharpay. I was born August 4, 1962. I am your niece and you are my Aunt Eugenia."

Still unable to speak, Eugenia muttered something, Lilly asked," Did you hear me? Are you all right?"

"I'm all right. I'm all right. I heard what you said, but give me a minute, here."

"Sure, Aunt Eugenia."

She heard the "Aunt Eugenia," but it took the words revolving round and round in her head before she could smile and realize all of the ramifications of those words. Perhaps there was something left in her life after all.

"What did you say your name was, dearie?"

"I am Lilly."

"You are Lilly?"

"Yes, Aunt Eugenia."

"How did you find me? How did you know about me? How did you know about Fields?"

"I know about you through Sunshine."

"I know Sunshine."

"She was contacted by an old friend, Star Hershing. Do you remember her?"

"Oh, yes, I do."

"Star told Sunshine how to contact my mom and me. That's how we found out about you."

"Where are you?"

"I am way out on the east coast, and you are all the way out west. We are so far away from each other but I needed to call. I was so nervous, but I'm glad I did."

"I'm glad you did. How old are you, Lilly?"

"I am getting closer to fifty."

"Oh, do you have children?"

"Yes, Aunt Eugenia, I do."

Sunshine Epstein

◻◼◻ ◼◻

"DON'T JUDGE PEOPLE BY THEIR RELATIVES."

Who am I who loves so dearly after so many years? Has Fields become a hero to me, to his family and now, the next generation? A hero is perhaps a person who dies for a noble cause, a fallen warrior. Fields is the fallen hero to the many of us whose lives he touched. Then, we have to consider what act or acts of bravery Fields did to be given this hero status. He was kind, helpful to children, a loving, family-oriented person and a wonderful lover.

How does that give him a hero's place in history? It doesn't, except for the fact that when a person dies, especially one who dies before his life has really begun, he becomes larger than life, larger than his deeds, and is loved for more than him self.

Through the years, Fields became my anchor. The times we spent together taught me to seek out those who naturally radiate happiness, and go into the world with joy and trust. We learned together that life is just a series of transformations. Perhaps his death was the greatest transformational lesson for those he left and for those who will come after. I learned an appreciation for another human soul as it lay next to mine, and how the souls of all of us intertwine and become part of the forest of the universe.

One afternoon in Buena Vista Park, Fields said, "You know, Sunshine, some people are trees and some are vines."

"So who are trees?"

"Tooty is a tree. He is planted straight into the ground. He has roots, you know, the kind that grow into other people's backyards."

"Who else is a tree?"

"You are. You spread your branches, your limbs and your arms far into the horizon. You are so high up there."

"You are high up there, too."

"Yep."

I asked, "Okay, who is a vine?"

"Your sister Marilynn is a vine. She is sort of a clinger. She grows up just when and where you don't want her."

"That's a good one. I know another one, your sister Eugenia. She creeps and trails around things, and then when the season is over, she just wilts and leaves her stems wrapped tightly around."

"You've got it."

"What would you say about ferns?"

"Ferns dot the forest floor, keeping the moisture from evaporating into nothingness. They are the life of the forest, right?"

"Who is a fern?"

"We are," he said

"We are, I agree."

In idolizing Fields and glorifying all that we shared, I have canonized him, and our life together. The moments we shared have allowed me to furnish and accept life's joyful moments, as well as to endure my moments of angst. One of the offerings Fields' death gave to all who loved him was the moments we needed to slow down and realize that we have missed him.

The memory of Fields is a gift that gives me permission to stop for a moment's glance at something that would have passed by unnoticed. All through the years without Fields, I have known he is here with me; it's as if he speaks to me through veils and whispers. When I am alone, I am not alone.

Recently, I had the good fortune and pleasure to travel to Warsaw, Poland. When I deplaned and walked out into the sunshine of that land, a breeze surrounded me; my hair blew in that breeze, and it was as if I was being hugged and hugged. I smiled. Hundreds of people were there in that receiving hall, but my hair was the only hair blowing, and I was the only one smiling. I felt a greeting of love and protection. I felt a special kind of tingling that would come and go as I traveled through the countryside. The whispering guidance could be none other than my Fields.

I went on with my life when Fields died but I have

always looked back. Looking back has given me the wisdom of time and the clarity of that I needed as I grew into womanhood. Womanhood wears many hats. First, we start as someone's daughter. We play that role well in the beginning because we love our creators. Then we move out into the world, acquire new experiences that make up our existence, and strive to become what society dictates. We come and go in the world of measured successes.

Each generation has outlined the dictates of true womanhood and it remains, to this day in constant flux. The young woman becomes a sister, thereby opening up the possibilities of becoming an aunt. Sisterhood works itself out and manifests in varying degrees of love and hate towards siblings. I have been a good sister, but not always perhaps in the eyes of my sibling. Being a successful person in most aspects of one's life makes it hard to admit failure.

Becoming a wife constitutes more than I can include here. Each of you who have become a wife or have taken one can fill in the story. It's an all-encompassing role that needs no more words. Motherhood is a fiercely given love that never ends until they put you into the crypt, vault or whatever arrangements are made for your physical remains.

Woman as a professional has to be a juggler--has to juggle not only all of those domestic hats, but also those that float out the professional arena. Man as a professional has to be a juggler as well. His juggling takes on other realms, but ideally must include domesticity. Being a grandmother is like everything in unison, the culmination of a life lived to the fullest. Being a grandfather is somehow facing today's generation and comparing it to prior lives. Grandfathers are a highlight in the generational atmosphere and are important curators of memories. With his memory for detail, Fields would have been an excellent grandfather.

I started volunteering at the Children's Hospital because a friend of mine had a grandchild who was born missing so much of what would give her a real life. At first, I just visited my friend's granddaughter, and then I found myself visiting others in residence to see if I could help them. Lena was a compelling young lady I met at the Children's Hospital during my volunteer shift. Her mother told me that next year Lena would be transferring to the regular hospital because she would no longer fit into the age criterion.

Lena told me she sees many things and no one believes her. She told me I looked like a movie star and I was going to write hundreds of books. I listened to Lena for many hours.

One particular day, as soon as I arrived at the hospital for my volunteer shift, I went directly to her room to tell her she was right about angels. The room was darkened and hushed voices came from the murky, gloomy interior. I was so anxious to tell Lena that I had seen an angel on my way to the hospital, but when I arrived she was gone. Lena was the angel I saw; I'm convinced it was she. She laid her hand on my shoulder and brushed by my cheek, letting me know she would make sure I had a safe journey through this life and into the next. She promised she would come back to get me when it was my time to go.

It was unbearable for me to think she was dead. Her lifeless body was lying on the bed while her family stared at her. Lena was the sweet dessert for some of my days, and Fields, as it has turned out, was the sweetest dessert of my life. These two, bound to me in love and death, rely on me to keep their memories alive. They, through me and now through you, can drift through the atmosphere like specks of dust looking for places to land.

The things Lena told me have saved my life, guided me and kept me safe. I will tell you what she told me so your life will be safe and you will be guided and protected, too.

Things Lena Told Me

"SOMETIMES YOU GET AND SOMETIMES YOU GET GOT."

I told Lena about Fields and I told her I needed her help to stop the aching. She told me to write a book about Fields and all my love for him. She said that I had to tell it from my heart and to go way down deep into my toes to bring up all of the things I remembered. She said if I bring it up from my toes, my body and my blood will have cured it, and, by the time the story came out, it would be a song with a melody we could sing over and over again. So I did.

Lena said many valuable things during the long conversations we had before she died. When she and I talked, the time would go from day to evening without notice. She was more than 50 years my junior, yet we dealt from the same deck on the same level. There is no replacement for living a long time but there are pockets where you can uncover a delightful and ageless lust for life at any age. I felt that most of the time Lena was my senior when it came to wisdom. I will never know if she realized she was going to die. Everyone else knew she was terminally ill but she never gave the slightest indication that she might not be here the next time I came to visit. She was a positive and strongly piercing person. What she said drilled a hole into my heart and filled it with prescriptions for living positively, healing the scar tissue of my many jagged encounters and offering tools to sooth the aches.

I have found in Lena and her wisdom bits and pieces of Fields? Fields had no idea his end was in sight but he certainly was as positive and as piercing a person as Lena. Lovely, ailing and failing Lena did for me what Fields had always done. She soothed and smoothed my thinking and eased my life's torments.

Lena asked me, "Do you buy green bananas,

Sunshine?"

"Yes, Lena, sometimes, well, usually I do because I think they will last longer."

"That's just it. You see, I would only buy bananas that are exactly ready,"

"Why?" I asked.

"Because when you get a banana that is ready, you are ready, too. If you buy something you have to wait for, you spend lots of your life waiting. If you are waiting, are you really living now? Just think about it."

"I guess I am waiting. I think I am waiting too much of the time, Lena. I won't ever buy green bananas again, you can be sure of it."

"Do you have clothes in your closet that still have tags on them?"

"Yes, madam, I do."

"That's a green banana, waiting to be worn and it means you have too many clothes because some are waiting to be worn."

"You're right. I buy clothes, put them in my closet and wait for a time to wear them. But instead of wearing them, I just buy more and put them in there to wait."

"No new clothes, Sunshine, until you have worn all those that are waiting with the tags still attached."

" Okay, I agree, but I will still have to think about this one."

Lena said, "When you think about it, we don't need most of the things we have. I don't need anything in here; I just need my gown and I need to feel good. I don't even remember what is in my closet or in my dresser drawers. Do you know what's in yours?"

"For sure I don't."

I went home that night and looked through my drawers. I found a ring that had been missing for years and years. I brought it to the hospital the next day and gave it to Lena.

Lena asked," Did you clean out all of your drawers?"

"Nope, just the top ones."

"Hey, if you find a warm pair of gloves, bring them in because my hands get so cold."

I got into those drawers in a big way and brought a great pair of warm gloves to Lena, but she was gone. I hung onto those gloves; they're still waiting, waiting for Lena.

I remember another conversation I had with Lena that made me believe in blessing the whole of humanity, good and bad. We were talking about people who do nice things for you and she said, "Bless them all."

"Even the bad ones?" I said.

"Oh, definitely, when you bless the good ones, that is good, but when you bless the bad ones, too, you bless yourself."

So now I always say, "Bless them all."

Lena talked about the spiritual world as if she were as intimate with it and as if it were her own reality. She said that the world of others, as she called them, was invisible to most humans, and that was why they did not receive more help from the other side.

She said, "It is as if they come from another planet or universe, but they are really those spirits who came from us in the before and in the hereafter. It isn't what we know, but it's what we can sense and feel when we are very, very quiet. It is energy, the essential energy that brings things out of us and brings us into its force. You must let it flow through you. If you don't know it is there, then you don't open yourself up to it, and you will not know anything about it."

"Do you think they are souls of people who have left this physical world, or do you think there is something that we have never known on this earth?"

"It is inside of us. We stop, we relax, we are quiet, and we begin to see things. It is nothing you can tell anyone and everyone sees things differently. I do not know if they are people or souls of people, but I do see things that no one has told me about."

"Do you think they may be angels doing God's work?"

"No angles are a separate thing, but they connected to other things in the universe. This surrounding essence is warm and friendly; it is like us, but not of us. It is powerful and can help us if we get to know it better."

"How do I get into this essence?"

Lena said, "First, you have to make a spot where you can go to meet it. It doesn't come to you. You go to this spot. You count down, three, two, one, and when you are one the platform, you open the door and you are there. It is a room and you go inside. I decorated my room with purple velvet and golden fringes. You can decorate your room with any colors using any style. It all happens when I am in the room and it is quiet. This room is my secret personal spot. When I'm done I leave the room, close the door, step out on the platform, and walk up the steps, one, two, three to the outside. This quiet option of being in your own room is open to everyone of us."

"Do you think you hypnotize yourself?"

Lena replied, "If I do, then that is what gets me to the place where I understand more of myself. I know I will see you in that place someday and I know we will help each other. Sort of like we are doing now, but it will be different, it will be like a melody, like a sunset, like a good meal--satisfying."

"Lena, do you think this is what they mean by the afterlife."

"No, it is life right now on double, triple, probably quadruple and more planes. It is happening right now or we would not be able to know it."

"Do you believe in time travel?"

"No, not really. Since we are on double, triple, and quadruple planes of life at the same time, we think those planes are time dimensions, but they are not. We cannot travel back and forth in time, past and future. We just have right now but there are pockets of time from the past, like bubbles. Sometimes they pop and we can see time in the past flowing out; it's only a moment or two, yet it's real."

The last time I saw Lena, she told me this story. It is word for word because I taped her telling it to me.

"Once there was a rice farmer and he had lots of land. He knew that he was ill. He knew that his time would come to die and he wanted to leave his land to the child who would make the best use of it. Most of his friends had sons which made choosing the one to carry on easier. This farmer had four daughters, no sons, and each had convincing reasons why they would be excellent rice farmers.

The father pondered a long time, and then decided to give each daughter three plump ripe grains of rice. He gathered them together and told them that he wanted them to have his life's treasure and proceeded to give them each a packet with the three grains of rice in it. He made it clear that this was the greatest gift he could give to them, and that it was his fondest hope they would cherish the gift as much as he cherished giving it.

"Each daughter bowed in front of her father and returned home. The first daughter thought this was a worthless gift and threw the three grains away immediately. The second daughter had the village jeweler put the three grains in a beautiful locket and she wore the locket everyday without fail. The third daughter had a wooden box carved and fitted the bottom with soft cotton, which was where she kept the precious grains of rice. The fourth daughter planted the grains of rice and each successive year harvested the crop. Each year the crop became bigger and better.

"One day, the father called them all together once again. He explained that he was very ill and would die soon. He then asked each to tell him what they had done with the rice grains he had given them. The first daughter confessed that she had thrown them out. The second daughter proudly showed her father the locket containing the three grains of rice. The third daughter opened the magnificently carved box and showed her father that she had kept the grains of rice safe. The fourth daughter asked that they all come to see what she had done with her grains of rice. By then, she had beautiful and productive fields of rice. She thanked her father for providing her with the tools to become fruitful.

"The father complimented his daughters on their decisions regarding the three grains of rice. 'But,' he said, 'I am giving all my property to my fourth daughter because she showed ingenuity and foresight in planting the grains of rice.'"

"Lena where did you hear this story?"

"My father told it to me."

The Transformation

■■■ ■■

"TALK SLOWLY, THINK QUICKLY."

In my mind I heard the question, "It might be nice if you told us your story, Sunshine. So many others have told you theirs; why not yours?"

I do not remember much about my beginning and the formative years. I hardly remember the faces of my early mother and father. I remember my mother eating cheese and my father smoking a cigarette in the den. I remember my mother driving anxiously in spurts and jerks, taking me across town to the orthodontist. I remember my father coming home from work, changing his shoes in the laundry room, and saying a smiling hello to everyone. We would all gather around the table, Lilly our housekeeper was serving us our dinner and my mother making me eat my broccoli first. Oh, how horrid. I remember a few rainy days, gloomy, damp and hopeless, and the dripping hibiscus tree in front of our den window.

Our neighbor to the east of us was Mrs. Jones who was without a Mr. Jones for the 25 years she lived next door to my family. The neighbor to the west, next to the house the Fields family once occupied, was Mrs. Watkins who lived in that house all of the time I knew her without a Mr. Watkins. Both widows showered their powers over me. Mrs. Watkins fashioned forget-me-nots on the bottoms of little hand-painted cups and saucers, and Mrs. Jones gave me photos of herself. I kept her photos in my upper right hand dresser drawer. One day, I got them all out and lined them up; I realized they were a perfect chronology of her life.

I remember State Street School, Gage Avenue School and Huntington Park High School. Is that why I became a teacher, or did I become a teacher because my mother said I would be good at it? Two things I wanted in a job was to have people look up to me and to have someone to look up to. When things got rough and while people still looked up to me, there was no one for me to look up to, so I started looking up to myself. That changed my life and allowed me a personal freedom. Everyone's personal freedom will manifest itself differently, but start looking up to yourself and you will find out who you really are; you're guaranteed to learn something new.

I know why I have saved nickels, pennies and dimes all of my life. It was because Lilly told us, "A penny saved is a penny earned." That simple philosophy was richly important to me. I have always driven a car that was fully paid for before I got behind the wheel. My father believed you didn't buy what you couldn't pay for. I was able to buy a new car when I needed it because I paid into a car account all of my working days. When I realized it held more than I needed for occasional new cars, I took money out to travel and learn. I still am making payments into my car account; I guess my heirs will inherit it.

I wish I could tell Lilly that the more I took out of that account the bigger it grew. After a while, the money just started to save itself. I wish I could tell her that as I have lived my life, I wonder if the things I do and have done are for me or for my heirs. Why do I still gather trinkets and assemble them when there is enough to go around the family several times? Who are my heirs? What makes them so all-powerful, so supreme that I imagine them in their radiant futures? Are we so tied into our past habits that we are unable to break with them until we are underground?

I have lived my life as I would live it again, but I would not have wanted Fields to die so young. I still feel I am on a waiting list and just standing in line. I am an old lady now, certainly by government standards, because they want to help me out. The older I get, the more they want to help with their bureaucratic programs. Isn't that nice? I always knew that my Uncle Sam would take care of me. I noticed the other day that going up the stairs was an awfully big effort. I felt out of breath even though I went up on all fours. My family wants to help me. They come over, bring food and do things they did not do when their dad was alive.

I never told their father about Fields because I felt he would not understand our relationship. I was afraid the story of Fields, the memory of him and how I loved him, would have changed some of the feelings my husband had for me. I never approached the subject and he never knew to ask.

I went to the post office today and stood in a very long line. The longest line was for passports. I was grateful that the mailing line was considerably shorter because standing for me as it is has become a challenge. After a while, it was my turn. I had six 10 by 13-size envelopes to send. The postmistress looked at them, frowned at me and said, "Why did you address these this way?"

I answered, "Did I do something wrong?"

She said, "No one else addresses them this way, you are supposed to write across the envelope."

This is where I instantly re-lived the lessons of vertical verses horizontal.

"No one ever told me how to address them before. Are you sure no one else does it this way?" I said with my hand to my mouth in dismay.

"You are the only one I have ever seen who addresses a 10 by 13 envelope this way."

Well, if I had ever been looking for a sign of who I

am after these many long years, I just got it at the post office. No one else does it the way I do. It has always been
like that, and I have always been my own drummer. What
really makes me angry is that now that she told me how to
do it and now I know how to do it, will I be doing it like
everyone else? The truth is should I be told what to do
by people who go postal? I think I should just continue
being me. I like not doing things like everyone else; it is
a distinction and a way out. It makes me unique.

As we get older, we start to ponder. I began to ponder more and more, so I wrote to you. I wanted to tell you
something and I did. I wanted you to listen and you did.

Twenty-five years have come and gone since I asked
you to listen and now I am the listener. I hear the laughter
of my family as they meet and share lunch. The noise is
deafening until someone opens the door and half of them
go outside. I just counted 28 and the doorbell is ringing.
More of my family will be joining the fold for lunch. I
used to be able to prepare food for all of them with my
eyes closed and my hands tied behind my back. Now everyone brings something. Why didn't I think of that a long
time ago?

Do these people know how they began in the old country? My great-grandfather called his shtetl, Grodno and now they call the land Belarus. I traveled back there once and the spirits of my ancestors greeted me and made me feel their love for me. They had a giant celebration in the city square with the greatest and longest fireworks show I had ever seen. In reality the city of Minsk had their anniversary celebration and was planned way before I came. I just made up that it was for my homecoming. I did not make up the part where I had a greeting. The spirits of people long ago came softly to let me know that they were safe. My mother's side of my family came from Kiev in the Ukraine. The spot where they lived long ago has been covered over with cement and buildings. I visited their spot and to me there was still a remaining essence that I welcomed. My father's side of my family immigrated to New York and then, San Francisco. My mother's side immigrated to Canada, to Boyle Heights and then Huntington Park. My children, grandchildren and great-grandchildren are all part of a new world and I am sinking into my own old world. I need to sit down more often. I check cereal boxes to count fiber content, but it doesn't seem to work anymore.

Some days I have a peaceful, yet hopeless chaos in my head. I cannot remember all of the things I want to recall, so I just close my eyes. If I do not see anything, I do not try to think so much. Everything for me has slowed down except the passing of days. I sit in my chair in my room and let time go by. When I bought this chair, I had a hard time deciding which chair would be perfect for me. I can still remember the salesman saying, "Sit in them, try them out and the one that you would be willing to spend the rest of your life in, that is the one you buy."

After breakfast, I felt like taking a nap, so I did. After lunch I took another nap. I remember when I was younger, there was a sixtieth wedding anniversary party for our friends. I sat next to a much older gentleman, really only a decade, but at that time he seemed much older. He asked me if I knew how to tell if I were getting old. I must have answered with something quite silly because he laughed and said, "Listen young lady, you know you are old when you start taking naps."

I have been on the permanent absentee ballot program for years and years. I guess you can do that when you are too old or too disabled to get to the neighborhood voting booths. Yesterday, I finally studied and attacked my absentee ballot. I looked at some of the names and then, studied a little about each of the candidates--issues. All of a sudden the voting game seemed quite overwhelming. I would like to go back and tell that older gentleman that you know you are old when you vote for cute names rather than actual ability. I had to put my foot down at the name, Bill Lower Taxes Welch. I did not vote for Bill and I took another nap.

As I See It

◻◼◻◼◻

"MY FAVORITE QUOTE: ALWAYS DRINK UPSTREAM FROM THE HERD."

Why does a flash of Tooty, darting behind a building and then peering out to see if someone has seen him appear in my mind so often? In my flash of Tooty, I see the building where Fields was killed. I ask myself to remember some of the times Tooty staged parties and family celebrations at Fields' gravesite. He was always saying prayers and asking for forgiveness. I do not think he was asking forgiveness for going off with another friend in a car, simply disappointing Fields. Is he asking more intensely and deeper because he knows his act was final and irreversible? Could Fields have stolen Florrie from Tooty who had been his first great love? Could Fields have somehow fouled up Tooty's chances of promotion at the plumbing parts factory where he had worked for years by his bad talk? Knowing Fields as I do, it is hard to believe that he would purposely hurt anyone. Is Tooty the one who is responsible for the decomposing corpse of his friend and mine, who lies beneath the ground at the very spot of Tooty's celebrations?

There is no legal or official proof of anyone's guilt over killing Fields. There never will be. The killing of Fields, my Fields, is only a flash that comes unannounced, the fleeting glimpse of Tooty darting behind a building, then peering out to see if someone has seen him. It is un-fitting that a person so powerful in the lives of those who love and loved him should be only a flash. Perhaps all of us are presently a flash, no more than the dewdrop that Pierce's Angel reflected upon. We have come to view the present as all we have, so let us encompass it in the here and now.

The purpose of Fields' life was to drop his seed to provide for his future generations. Tragically his future

was cut short but all that he learned and all of the preparations he made for the future were funneled through me. I
feel I have lived two lives in one. I have lived my life and I
have lived one for Fields. I have passed on his perceptions
and insights, mingled with my own.

When I finally decided that it was time to meet Lilly,
child of Fields, I needed to consummate my reality. In
passing the torch to Lilly, I hoped I would be able to meld
myself into one whole person. I have become, and I am
now, Sunshine Joy Epstein, a real person.

The Light

◻️◼️◻️ ◼️◻️

"NOW THAT YOU HAVE WRITTEN IT DOWN AND YOU ARE EXPECTING APPLAUSE, THROW IT OVER A MIGHTY CLIFF AND WAIT TO HEAR THE SOUNDS IT MAKES WHEN IT LANDS. THAT IS YOUR APPLAUSE."

There isn't much light at the end of her tunnel, not much light at all. Sunshine lies stuffed into a hospital bed that has become too thin for her bloated frame. She had prided herself on her ability to always keep her natural shape and never let it get out of hand. She even allowed herself an occasional delusion that she was thin and willowy. She ate only proper foods that could not and did not put an extra ounce on her frame. She is nearly gone now, but her worldly goods lay on the dining room table for those to recollect, take, buy, or exchange for a memory.

Fields is gone and she thinks of him in another dimension, floating and melting; they are together in that conjoined, rarified space looking down upon us who remember them.

Conversations from long ago come parading past Sunshine. Scenes from a previous life flicker and sparkle in and out of her mind; the family, young and old, friends, the students, art, travel, and special thoughts of her friend in life and death, her dear Fields--Fletcher Fields. She never called him Fletcher; his name is and always will be Fields. Everyone called him Fields, even his own mother.

The conversation Sunshine hears resounds in her head and formulates into this scene. It doesn't make sense to us, but Sunshine knows it is her history.

"I am a beatnik, not a hippie," she said.
Plain and simple, she's an original peacenik.

"What does this have to do with anything? Aren't we in the here and now? Aren't we? "

"Sure, but all the same, she was just a bum then."

"Well, bum or not, she has booked a flight to Central Transylvania."

"Where the hell is that?"

"Someplace in Romania where the old beatniks hang out."

"I'm going there."

"You're too old, chickadee."

"Am not."

"Are too."

Sunshine is still fighting for and against herself. She is letting herself know that she is here for the moment, but ready to go. She had given to this life the best she has to offer. Now her thoughts are mixed and sometimes frozen. She still wants to advise her family, and evaluate the behavior of her grandchildren so their parents have a stronger handle. She still wishes to be an integral part of their lives, but feels the fading and dimming as a certainty of dying and hallucinates as a finality of death. The flickering lights give way, and her mind creates an intricately designed yellow umbrella under which she stands; all of the components that make up Sunshine Epstein are there. A smile crosses her face and brilliance shines momentarily in her eyes as she recognizes she has accomplished her purpose.

She lies still. Arms and legs that are fully worn stretch for the last time. The lights have gone out for Sunshine and it comes as a welcome relief. As she melts from the room, her beloved grandmother, holding little Lena's hand, escorts her on one arm and the other arm is lovingly supported by Fletcher Fields. She is reporting for duty in another empirical realm.

467514

Made in the USA